YOU
JUMP
FIRST

YOU JUMP FIRST

~~~~~~~~~~~~

MYAH ARIEL

SIMON PULSE

NEW YORK   AMSTERDAM/ANTWERP   LONDON
TORONTO   SYDNEY/MELBOURNE   NEW DELHI
~~~~~~~~~~~~

SIMON PULSE
An imprint of Simon & Schuster Children's Publishing Division
1230 Avenue of the Americas, New York, New York 10020
For more than 100 years, Simon & Schuster has championed authors and the stories they create. By respecting the copyright of an author's intellectual property, you enable Simon & Schuster and the author to continue publishing exceptional books for years to come. We thank you for supporting the author's copyright by purchasing an authorized edition of this book.
No amount of this book may be reproduced or stored in any format, nor may it be uploaded to any website, database, large language model, or other repository, retrieval, or artificial intelligence system without express permission. All rights reserved.
Inquiries may be directed to Simon & Schuster, 1230 Avenue of the Americas, New York, NY 10020 or permissions@simonandschuster.com.
First Simon Pulse edition June 2026
Text © 2026 by Simon & Schuster, LLC
Cover illustration © 2026 by Katie Smith
All rights reserved, including the right of reproduction in whole or in part in any form.
SIMON PULSE and colophon are registered trademarks of Simon & Schuster, LLC.
For information about special discounts for bulk purchases, please contact
Simon & Schuster Special Sales at 1-866-506-1949 or business@simonandschuster.com.
Simon & Schuster strongly believes in freedom of expression and stands against censorship in all its forms. For more information, visit BooksBelong.com.
The Simon & Schuster Speakers Bureau can bring authors to your live event. For more information or to book an event, contact the Simon & Schuster Speakers Bureau at 1-866-248-3049 or visit our website at www.simonspeakers.com.
Book design by Tiara Iandiorio
The text of this book was set in Minion Pro.
Manufactured in the United States of America
10 9 8 7 6 5 4 3 2 1
Library of Congress Control Number 2025046601
ISBN 9798347106882 (hc)
ISBN 9798347106875 (pbk)
ISBN 9798347106899 (ebook)

For Kelsey, Allison, and Amy.
I'm so glad our friendship didn't
peak in high school.

And for every friend who's helped
a friend through heartbreak.
You deserve all the emotional
support you give and more.

L ast year, I kissed Patrick Ling on the final day of our summer at the lake. The moment had been *years* in the making, and I'd expected nothing short of pure cinema magic—music only we could hear, pyrotechnics in the distance, a round of deafening applause from our friends, family, random passersby . . .

But fate, or something like it, intervened, and I only got about four seconds of uninterrupted mouth-to-mouth before *Animals Gone Wild* crashed my first real shot at living out the friends-to-lovers plotline I'd been dreaming up in my head since eighth grade.

I met Patrick when his parents bought the house next to my family's at the end of the cul-de-sac on Big Bear Lake's south shore. Like me, Patrick was awkward and gangly, and we both had lisps, courtesy of our upper and lower retainers. I like to think we bonded over our shared struggle words: *sunscreen* and *swimsuits*. On top of that, we were both sporty. He was into baseball. I was into soccer. We were, obviously, destined to fall in love.

And we both had fun pissing off Tommy—his older, "too cool" brother—with our version of hilarious pranks, like the time we threw one of my red socks into the wash with all his white tees, or when we swapped his mouthwash for vinegar. Tommy was just a year ahead of us, but he acted like being on the planet approximately four hundred days longer gave him permission to do things like refer to me as Patrick's "little friend" instead of by my name, Andie. While Tommy was always a part of the group, he had this way of hanging at the edge of our circle, taking it all in. He's like this weird, angsty puzzle I could never quite figure out. He also had a habit of doing this thing where he'd look at me for long stretches of time, almost daring me to stare back. And, look, I'm stubborn. Just ask my best friend, Mel. But you can only ignore green eyes for so long. Whenever I'd give in and look up at Tommy, he'd just grunt, slam his laptop shut, and go off somewhere to practice pitching while blasting Post Malone.

But Patrick, he and I clicked the day my mom strongly

suggested I cross the lawn to "help the new boys next door" unpack their kitchen supplies while she brought over a carafe of sangria for their mom. From that day on, I'd been waiting for our moment—the one when all of that "clicking" would turn into *more*. All our friends seemed to be waiting for it too.

Then finally last summer, after weeks of enough *will they, won't they*s between me and Patrick to drive Mel up a wall and keep an e-reader bursting at its seams, it finally happened.

It was our last day at the lake. The day before we'd all be packing up and heading home to get ready for the school year. For a final hurrah, our group went down to Boulder Bay with our paddleboards, Frisbees, and picnic baskets. It was eighty degrees at golden hour, and like every year by this time, we were a little summered out—bored of lazing around in the sun and ready to get back to our hometowns and the busy lives we lived there—but still somehow not ready to let each other go. We took turns tossing a Frisbee on the sun-baked beach and cooling off in the sapphire-blue water.

"You need to put your big-girl panties on and make the first move," Mel said while we were out in the water straddling our boards, a safe distance out of the boys' earshot.

I was telling her about the night before, when I'd spent an hour on my porch with Patrick. How he'd looked at me with his deep sable eyes and said the single best thing I've probably ever heard: *I think you're my favorite person to talk to, Andie.*

I was speechless, the silence between us filled with terrifying, wonderful possibilities. I just knew he was going to kiss me then and there. I was half a second from closing my eyes and leaning in myself. But like a record scratch, his mom called out from their porch, "Patrick! Your dad needs help on the grill, and I can't find Tommy to save my life!"

Patrick sighed, looked at me, and reached up to brush the curls out of my face. Seconds later, he was gone.

"Jeez, Mrs. Ling! Talk about a cockblock," Mel said, before splashing herself with water to cool down. She pinned me with a serious look. "At this point, Andie, it's basically now or never. We all leave tomorrow. Like my dad says, you have to shit or get off the pot."

"Ew, okay," I told Mel. "I did *not* need that visual."

She wasn't wrong, though. As my feet dangled in the cool water and the sun beat down on my bare back, I turned to the shore and there he was. Patrick. Alone on a beach towel.

The goal was clear. He was leaving tomorrow, sure. But if I kissed him today, we could spend the next ten months becoming *more* to each other. He could visit me in Santa Monica and go to my games and take me to dances. And my parents could drive me up to Santa Barbara so I could do the same.

We could make it work until the next summer at the lake, our last before senior year. Then we'd go to college, and well, we'd figure that out too.

Mel wished me luck, and I paddled back to shore with my eyes on the prize. When I reached the sand, I shook out my hair, adjusted the triangle top of my kelly-green bikini, and tried to shake off the nerves. I'm not usually self-conscious in a two-piece bathing suit, but when Patrick watched me walk toward him, it felt like the look on his face in that one moment somehow held every single look he'd given me before, and still, in it, there was something *more*.

I sat down by his side and dried off with a spare towel, still trying to figure out what I could say to set the mood. For a second, I studied our sandy toes, the dusting of dark hair on his shins, the way the breeze blew the fabric of his trunks. I wanted to kiss him, but I wasn't ready to look at him just yet.

Patrick was the first to speak. "You know what I said last night? About how you're my favorite person to talk to? What if that doesn't have to end after tomorrow like it always does? What if we don't wait until next summer to . . ."

Patrick's words trailed off. I turned toward him, and I'm not sure if I groaned or whimpered from being left hanging, because instead of using his mouth to find his words, he used it to find mine.

His lips brushed ever so slightly against mine, and next his fingers were threaded through my wet hair. This was it. I was finally kissing Patrick Ling, fully and completely. I let myself bask in the moment. With one hand, I gripped the sun-bleached beach towel beneath us, and with the other,

I clutched his wet T-shirt. He smelled exactly as he always had—like lemon and trees and a tiny hint of clean sweat—but concentrated by one thousand.

Suddenly there was heavy panting. Then I felt something cold and slimy land on my knee. For a split second I thought maybe Patrick was trying out a new, questionable move on me. I was weirded out, sure, but prepared to go with it.

Then he pulled away mid-kiss.

"Hey, old girl, what you got there?" he said sweetly.

Thoroughly confused by this odd attempt at seduction, I opened my eyes and spotted Maisy, Tommy's French mastiff, planted firmly between us. To my horror, she held a dead fish in her mouth—with its slime *dripping onto my leg*. With a wet *thwack* she dropped the fish into my lap.

A noxious stench filled my nostrils. And I have never been credibly accused of having a strong stomach. I gagged, and it was like my soul was trying to escape my body.

Grimacing, Patrick grabbed the fish and flung it over his shoulder. Then he yelled over my head, "What the hell, Evan! I thought you had her!"

I shot to my knees, desperate to remove myself from the smell, the embarrassment, possibly life itself. But instead of an escape, I found myself bathed in a tall dark shadow, framed by the late-afternoon sun.

"Oh, *shit*." Tommy Ling kneeled to meet my eyes. He was panting from chasing Maisy, and his stare was intense. Eyes green and bright, with dark wet strands of his hair plastered across his scrunched-up brow. I glanced down at his full lips just as he said, "My bad, Andie. You okay?"

I was still gagging as our friend Evan jogged forward, taking in the scene. "Duuude," he said to Tommy before covering his mouth. "I thought *you* had her!"

Mel miraculously appeared from the water, filling out our audience. "You look green, girl. Are you . . . are you gonna puke?"

Mortified, I shook my head. "Ummm"—grunt—"I think"—dry heave—"it's fine. I'm g—" Cough. "I'm good." I tried to sound as convincing as possible while trying to keep my insides, well, on the inside. But one look down at the fish guts still dripping off my lap, and I was doomed.

Mel, angel that she is, saw the incoming disaster before anyone else. "All right, everybody!" she chirped. "Let's give the girl some space!" She shooed everyone, Patrick included, away and helped me stumble to the water to rid myself of fish entrails.

Later that night, I locked myself in my room with my "Crashing Out" playlist on a loop. I traded spinning around to Robyn's "Dancing on My Own" for lying flat on my bed listening to Lizzy McAlpine—the final moments of summer slipping away as I cried into my ears. And as Lizzy's lyrics shook the walls of my room, and probably gave my mom ample reason to worry, like a crazy person I started to laugh through the tears. Because Patrick Ling had *finally* kissed me. But the whole thing had played out more like an *SNL* sketch than the start of a date-night movie.

Then, like it had been doing all night while I'd been in the throes of an emotional breakdown, my pillow vibrated. I reached over and opened my text thread with Patrick, showing the two messages he'd sent after the beach that I'd ignored.

6:25 p.m.

Patrick: hey just checking on u

8:05 p.m.

Patrick: we're heading back down the mountain

And the latest one that I was *really* not equipped to deal with.

11:02 p.m.

Patrick: so that kiss . . . we gonna talk about it?

I was officially the Worst. And maybe I let the sting of humiliation keep me from responding to Patrick for too long, because when I finally did, he left me on read.

"You did *not* send this to Patrick Ling." Mel's hazel eyes practically bulge out of their sockets as she gapes at me from the foot of my bed, holding the evidence that I did, in fact, *send this to Patrick Ling.*

"Wait," she says, dragging her thumb across my screen. A second later, her face scrunches and she's smacking a palm to her forehead. "Too late! Can't unsend it now!" She tosses the phone onto the bed.

We're in my room at the lake house, where we arrived about an hour ago. I'd planned to call Mel when I got upstairs, but as soon as Mom and I pulled into the driveway of our A-frame, Mel skipped across the street and climbed the stone steps of our porch to greet us. Like always, she looked casually cool in a vintage tee and denim cutoffs. But now her typical waist-length strawberry-blond hair had been chopped into a chin-length bob and was a few shades darker. I'd have been shocked if she hadn't video-chatted me through the entire cut-and-color appointment for moral support.

We had both decided that senior year was the perfect time for a "brand refresh." She picked a bold hair style, and I guess I just decided to . . . be bold.

Melissa Bridges has been my best friend since the third grade. During the school year, she lives in Colorado with her parents, who both teach law at CU Boulder. But their winter/summer vacation house sits right across from ours on Lakefront Drive. And since we were nine, from every June to August, plus the occasional Christmas and spring break, we've shared every item of clothing and secret imaginable.

It takes about three seconds for me to give her a Patrick update and 0.3 seconds for her to lose her shit.

I'm sitting, knees tucked on the mattress, wondering if my dramatic friend is just being . . . well, dramatic. "Is it really *that* bad?"

"Catastrophic," she says before doing an elaborate turn on her heel and falling backward to land beside me.

I pick up the phone from where it landed on my purple

comforter. One tap at the screen uncovers my apparent crime—a text I sent to Patrick Ling while my mom was driving us up the mountain to our lake house for the start of our summer vacation.

Me: Hey Patrick! U know our kiss last summer? Maybe tonight we can try that again!

Me: And more . . . ♥

Okay. Upon further inspection, maybe she's not overreacting. "I can see how I might have taken being bold a little too far," I admit—this time falling back to lie next to her. It had taken me forever to craft what I considered the perfect icebreaker to rekindle our connection after Fishgate and reverse my ghosting debacle. But after a half hour of workshopping it, my thumbs were sore, my brain was scrambled, and I just decided to—quite literally—send it. A *big* mistake, apparently.

"And more?" Mel says, turning her face to inspect my profile with a grimace. "Almost a year of radio silence, and you break the ice with a sext? Andrea Cassandra Weaver, I did not think you had it in you."

When she puts it that way, I have no choice but to hide my face with my hands. "Ughhhh . . . ," I groan. "What are the odds he thinks I meant something mild . . . like tongue?"

"About the same as your odds of mating with a thousand-year-old vampire and birthing hybrid offspring," she deadpans.

"Time for you to stop rewatching *Twilight*," I say. I flip onto my stomach, burying my face in the comforter.

When it comes to sex, Mel knows I've got a vivid imagination—we have a mutual affinity for smutty fanfic, after all. But she also knows that when it comes to real life, I'm a late bloomer. Even though heading into senior year with my virginity intact isn't something I'm particularly embarrassed about, propositioning my yearslong crush via text message absolutely is.

It's not like I haven't had opportunities to, as my mom puts it, "explore" in that department. But every time I've gotten *almost* there with somebody, we've crashed and burned. There was my first kiss the summer after seventh grade with Everett Walker. We were on my parents' pontoon boat, and before our lips connected, our braces clashed, leaving me with two fat lips and a gnarly sunburn. Fast-forward to my Spring Fling date this year with Dennis Masters. He was a perfect gentleman the whole night—brought me pink roses and a couple of cans of sparkling rosé because he knows I'm not a fan of beer. I was charmed enough that after the dance we made out in the back of his Bronco. But just when hands started to venture toward zippers and buttons, it was like someone on a megaphone had screamed, *He's not Patrick!* And suddenly everything felt all wrong. Call me a hopeless romantic with an overactive inner world, but what's so special about a "first time" if it's not going to be with the first person who's made you feel the things you've only read about or seen in movies?

But judging by both Mel's reaction *and* the pit in my stomach, my powers of seduction are majorly lacking.

"What if I tell Patrick I was hacked?" I mumble into the duvet. Then, looking up, I confess, "You know how I get when it comes to him. Just being friends who flirt was easy, but *now*?" My hands flail in the direction of my phone. "The dead-fish incident was bad enough!"

"I know. Lucky for you, I'm basically a pro at this," she says, squaring her shoulders. "We can fix it. We just have to get serious. You show up to the party looking bangin'. I'm talkin' Rihanna-on-a-red-carpet-level swag, and if Patrick mentions the text, you brush it off like it's no big deal. He'll be so entranced by your hot confidence that he'll feel weird for questioning it."

I turn back over, and for a few quiet moments, we simply stare at the swirling ceiling fan. I'm imagining the spinning blades conjuring a spell to send me back in time two hours before I sent the text.

"Earth to Andieeeee." Mel's words puncture my trance. "I'm gonna need you *fully* committed to pull this off. If not, you'll walk into this totally underprepared, and then we're dealing with . . . " She pauses. She settles on "With DEFCON 3!"

I roll my eyes at her. "Do you even know what that means?" I ask.

"I know enough," she says. "Look, the Lings' Summer

Kickoff party is in two hours. And after this"—she picks up the phone again—"no more improv for you!"

"Okay, fine," I say before rolling off the bed to stare at the suitcases I'm supposed to be unpacking. "I guess we can start by figuring out what we're going to wear." I take a deep breath. Everything is going to be fine.

"That's more like it." Mel winks at me.

As I start piling my clothes on the bed, I hear Mom banging around in the kitchen. When we arrived, it took her a few seconds of fiddling with the keys to open the lock to the front door. She tried to laugh it off, but I could see right through her. So far, she has tried to play it cool, but she didn't fool me with the game of Heartbreak Karaoke she initiated on our drive up the mountain.

This is our first trip to the lake house since Mom and Dad's divorce became official in March. From now on, winters on the mountain are his, summers are hers, and I'm still figuring out how to love this place with only two-thirds of the people who make it feel like home.

With its high ceiling, cedar beams, and wood-burning fireplace, our lake house has always had the coziest feel. And Mom's love of thrifting means that none of the furniture matches, but somehow it all still works. But this time, it feels colder—even with the bright sun streaking through the windows that overlook the lake. It feels like something big is missing here. Or maybe just someone.

"So . . . how exactly am I supposed to approach a person who's potentially still ignoring me?" I ask Mel while moving on to unzip my oversize duffle. I picture Patrick's face—his dark brown eyes, full lips, and the dimples that only show up when he's laughing or *really* happy. I wonder if they'll make an appearance when he sees me tonight. Usually we'd greet each other with huge smiles, his just slightly crooked. Then we'd hug, and he'd squeeze tight and say, *Hey, Andie-Bug.* And I feel like that alone could sustain me if I were ever stranded somewhere like on an island or a poop cruise. But the thought of all of this changing because of a dead fish, a light ghosting, and a misguided sext sends a pang of regret through my chest.

"Well, as mentioned, first you'll show up at the party looking unignorable," she says. "We're talkin' *real* hot-girl shit!"

I snort. Because my understanding of "hot" is how in those nineties movies, they give an already-gorgeous girl some contacts, a flat iron, and a strappy dress, and suddenly she's Hailey Bieber. I've already got perfect vision, and if I had to describe my hair, I'd just say it's "a lot," so flattening it takes the better part of a day. And even after applying tinted sunscreen, a dab of lip oil, and finger-curling this mane, I'm still just Andie. Sure, I've got Mom's dark freckles and Dad's hazel eyes—a combo I'm told makes me look *original*, whatever that means. But if there's something I can do to knock Patrick off balance when he sees me tonight after all the many times he's seen me before, I don't know what that is.

"Stop that!" Mel shouts before pelting me with a pillow from across the bed.

I duck just before it hits me in the face. "Stop what?" I ask, lobbing it back.

"Whatever's going on up here," she says, waving a hand around her face. "Repeat after me: I am Andrea Cassandra Weaver, and this summer, I am up to real hot-girl shit and real hot-girl shit only."

I stare blankly at my best friend. "You can't be serious," I say.

"Dead serious." She wields another pillow and aims it at my head. "Now say it!"

I take a deep breath. "I am Andrea Cassandra Weaver, and this summer, I am up to real hot-girl shit and real hot-girl shit only."

"That's what I like to hear," Mel says. "Now toss me that halter dress with the low back."

And because right now Mel's got enough confidence for the both of us, I do exactly as she says.

The Lings' lake house has always looked like something from the cover of *Mountain Living* magazine. And as far as I know, it probably is. But when Sasha Ling dresses the place up for her annual Summer Kickoff party, it feels like it could have sprung to life from the pages of a storybook.

I am talking twinkling string lights stretched between the trees that bookend a multilevel deck. That same deck wraps around the house and overlooks the shore. Then there are white candle-lit lanterns sitting on gingham-clad picnic tables, and of course the flowers—blues, purples, and the fiercest shades of fuchsia hydrangeas, cut and placed in mason jars with little burlap bows for a rustic mountain feel. Patrick's mom knocks it out of the park every year. And I can't think of a more perfect setting for us to pick right up where we left things last summer on the beach. Just minus the part where I'm covered in fish guts.

With arms linked, Mel and I cross my yard and head over to the Lings' house at the end of the cul-de-sac, where soft music creates a moody soundtrack for our arrival.

"What is it with our parents' age group and their inability to let go of the eighties and the nineties?" Mel asks in mock disgust. "I mean, would it kill them to play something from this millennium, at least?"

"I don't know, I kind of like this song," I admit. It's got a sweeping charm—a fairy-like voice singing about dancing and kissing under a silver moon with fireflies floating around. It reminds me of those same nineties rom-coms I used to watch with Mom that Dad used to tease us about. Mom would lob handfuls of popcorn at him from our cozy spot on the couch, and he'd never fail to catch at least some of the pieces in his mouth.

Within seconds of breaching the front door, Sasha Ling has spotted us, and I'm no longer thinking about the past. "Oh my goodness, Mel, Andie! Don't you both look darling in your little getups? Let me guess . . . vintage?" she asks, referencing the flowy halter top I paired with a patchwork denim skirt, and Mel's tie-dyed romper—both finds we thrifted last summer.

"Yes, ma'am," Mel confirms as Mrs. Ling wraps her in a hug.

Even though the Lings make their year-round home up in Santa Barbara, Mrs. Ling hails from South Carolina. And if she doesn't remind you of that fact every third chance she gets, her strong Southern belle accent does the job for her. She and Mr. Ling met as freshmen at USC—he was starting center fielder for the Trojans men's baseball team, and she was a Song Girl—and they've been a power couple ever since.

"Where's that gorgeous mama of yours?" Mrs. Ling asks, turning to pull me into a hug. But before I can tell her my mom is coming late, she steps back, and the charm bracelet on my left wrist gets stuck in a long tendril of her honey-blond hair. I shoot a panicked look at Mel, who jumps in to help disentangle us.

"Oh, honey, just yank it," Mrs. Ling insists. "It's not mine, and I've got loads more where it came from."

At this point I notice the half-empty glass of champagne in her other hand, just as Mr. Ling joins us with his classic million-dollar smile. He might be going silver up top, but like his boys, he's tall and broad-shouldered—still sporty, too. Like he's taken the *once an athlete, always and athlete* motto to heart. "Looks like you ladies have already started trouble," he jokes, his good-natured laugh quickly turning into a grimace when he sees just how dicey his wife's current situation is.

"I can just take it off," I offer, desperate to get out of the tangle. Completely mortified, I scan the house praying that Patrick is nowhere in sight. This is not how our entrance was supposed to go—me snatching the wig off his mom's head less than a minute into the party. I unlatch the bracelet while Mr. Ling gingerly secures his wife's hair. When they're finally free from my wrist, the charms fall to dangle from one of the wavy layers of Mrs. Ling's wig, like a bohemian hair accessory. I have to admit, it has a certain flair.

"I'm so sorry, Mrs. Ling," I mumble, and she waves off the apology.

"Don't you worry, sweetheart. I'll get this back to you in the morning when I've had time to wrestle it out of this old thing. Till then, thanks for the bling!" She gulps down the remainder of her glass and sashays into the kitchen.

"Why don't you girls head out back?" Mr. Ling suggests warmly. "The crab boil is hot and ready, and I'm pretty sure Patrick's running around out there somewhere with all your lake buddies."

At the sound of Patrick's name, my stomach drops. The wig snafu made me forget for a moment that I'm on a damage-control-and-romance-rescue mission. So after making a pit stop in the bathroom to collect ourselves, Mel and I step outside onto the sweeping deck. I spot him in the distance, standing on the lawn by the water. He's wearing navy-blue board shorts and a casual white button-up with sleeves rolled three-quarters of the way up his arms. The warm rays of the almost-setting sun paint gold streaks across the floppy dark brown waves of his hair. If my eyes aren't tricking me, it looks like he's grown about an inch or two as well.

I forget Mel is next to me until she speaks. "Damn. That kid glowed up since last summer, didn't he?"

I release a nervous laugh but don't really have a response. The truth is, I've always loved looking at Patrick. Even when he was short and skinny. Even when he had braces and acne. "It's okay. We're okay," I say to Mel, but mostly to myself. "He looks good. I look good. I can do this."

"Yeah, you can!" Mel says before smacking me on the butt.

Side by side we begin our descent down the stairs. The entire time it feels like we're moving in slow motion, and I'm praying to the Summer Kickoff gods that I don't trip over my feet and fall flat on my face. The music has changed again to something jazzy about a girl named Valerie, and the tempo makes my heart race.

Patrick is talking with our small circle of friends, all of us brought together by the summers we've spent on the lake. There's Evan and Mason, Selina and Olivia. But one girl's unfamiliar face trips my radar for a moment. Has a new family joined our lake crew? Brushing it off, I try to stay focused on the casual, unbothered opening line Mel and I practiced—

*Hey, Patrick. *flicks hair over shoulder*

Simple. To the point. Un-mess-up-able.

As we get closer, I walk into Patrick's line of sight and make a point to widen my smile and wave. His return glance seems to stutter across my face before he drops his eyes to the ground. Then he looks up at me with a small timid half smile. This can't be good. I tilt my head toward Mel. "Did you see that?"

She frowns and shrugs, but grabs my hand and gently tugs me forward when I hesitate.

We reach the group, and it's like the sea parts, revealing Patrick to us in all his golden-toned glory. Ready for the plunge, I'm opening my mouth to deliver my well-practiced opening line, when my eyes pan down to notice that he's holding someone's hand. The girl with the unfamiliar face. He's holding her hand.

Whatever I was supposed to do and say vanishes into thin air. The grill explodes, and the Lings' pontoon boat sinks beside the dock. Everything about this picturesque storybook party goes haywire in my brain as I lay eyes on the person I am guessing is Patrick's surprise girlfriend.

"Heeeeey, Andie and Mel," Patrick's best friend, Evan, says, interrupting my fog of confusion. "Arriving fashionably late, I see." He gestures to our outfits, and suddenly everything I've done today feels like a major miscalculation. Mel is almost always meticulously styled, from her elaborate nail designs to her designer shoes. But today I let her dress me and questionably traded my typical basic sundress for a cropped halter and waist beads.

"Oh, you know us," Mel says, jumping in like the heroine she was born to be. "Gotta keep you all on your toes. I'm Mel, by the way." She extends her hand to the tall, model-esque girl whose silk-straight auburn hair looks like an ad for Pantene. "My family lives in the green house on the other side of the street."

Patrick's . . . friend gently shakes Mel's hand with her free one. "I'm Rebekah, but you can call me Bekah," she says, and her voice sounds raspy but smooth, like one of those late-night radio hosts Mom listens to sometimes. And now I'm wondering how girls our age get voices like that. Rebekah sounds mature *and* experienced, like she'd be the last person to be so embarrassed that she'd ghost her crush for months. "I'm staying here with Patty and his family for the summer," she adds.

At this, I cough. And not like a cutesy, demure *I just needed to clear my throat* kind of cough. It's an *I've swallowed a hair ball and might need the Heimlich* kind of cough. Because, first of all, who is Patty? Somebody's grandma? Second of all, Rebekah's living here for the summer? The Summer Kickoff gods need to be *so* for real right now.

I haven't managed to stop coughing. Mel thwacks me hard on the back while the object of my desire finally decides to speak.

"H-hey, Andie," Pat(ty?) says in a way that sounds like he's not so sure how to introduce his girlfriend to another girl he's kissed. "Hey, Mel."

"Heeeeeyyy, Patty," Mel says like she's announcing a game show, and I'd very much like to go to bed right this second and start all over again tomorrow. "So, Bekah, how long have you and Patrick been . . . ?" She stops short of finishing the sentence and just gestures toward their still clutched hands.

"Since the fall." Rebekah looks over at Patrick for confirmation, and all he can do is nod. "I moved down to Santa Barbara from the Bay this year, and we met on the first day of calc."

"That's great!" I offer, having rediscovered my voice. So, practically days after our disastrous kiss, while I was still crashing out over Patrick, he was being seduced by raspy-voiced Rebekah?

Panicked, I realize we need to change the game plan. Because if Patrick is now with someone else—and I'll deal with the tidal wave of heartbreak threatening to drown me later—that makes my text *so* much worse. Worse than Mel and I originally feared. After a quick glance at Mel, I say to Bekah, "I'm really, *really* happy for you. Listen, Patrick! By any chance, did you get a text from me today? I was hacked earlier, so I'm just . . . you know . . . I'm just checking around." I reach up to scratch the back of my neck because suddenly I've broken out in what feels like hives. I only hope no one else can see them.

"Oh yeah, anybody else here get a text from Andie?" Mel

asks with pitch-perfect concern. "I got, like, five. Real wild stuff, too! Hackers these days are out of control."

The whole group stares at Mel and me like we've sprouted branches from our foreheads. And honestly, if that did happen, it might be less weird than the last five minutes we've all experienced.

Patrick breaks the awkward silence by clearing his throat. "No, sorry," he says while swinging their clutched hands back and forth like a nervous tick. "Bekah and I have been running around all day helping Mom get the place set up. So I haven't really checked my phone since I got up this morning."

I could kiss the ground.

"Oh, really?" I say with a little too much enthusiasm. "Well. If you happen to have a text from me, feel free to delete it. Immediately. Don't even bother opening it. Wouldn't want you to get scammed." I turn toward my friend. "Mel! What do you say we head upstairs for some of those crab legs?"

Mel agrees, and in the next moment, we are excusing ourselves to slink back upstairs and into the house.

Because now we've got a new mission—find *Patty's* phone. ASAP.

"Patrick's room is upstairs at the end of the hall," I whisper to Mel as we sneak our way through the party. We try to keep a low profile—heads down, no eye contact.

Once we're about halfway up the stairs, Mel grabs my arm. "Wait! If Rebekah's staying here for the summer, that means Mrs. Ling probably put her up in one of the boys' rooms, right?"

I deflate. "Good point," I concede.

This sends me into detective mode. I am picturing the layout of the Lings' enormous lake house. The primary suite where Glen and Sasha sleep is tucked away behind the kitchen on the main floor. Upstairs, Patrick and Tommy each have their own room. And downstairs, behind the rec room and in-house theater, there's a guest room with four bunk beds. Like Mel suggested, Mrs. Ling, with all her Southern hospitality, most likely put Rebekah up in Patrick's room for the summer—which means he's probably sleeping downstairs in a bunk.

For the past several seconds, while I've been standing on the stairs probably looking like some version of the blond-woman-trying-to-solve-hard-math meme, Mel's been staring at me. But now that I've had my light bulb moment, I grab her wrist, and we head to the lower level of the house.

When we finally make it downstairs, there are about a dozen partiers hanging around in various stages of enjoyment. Some play pool while others chat at the bar Mr. Ling renovated to look like an old Western saloon last summer. Thankfully, everyone's too preoccupied to notice the two of us sneaking around.

"Bunk room is our best bet," I whisper to Mel, realizing I haven't clued her in on my hunch. She's just blindly following me down the carpeted hallway past the Lings' theater. Classic movie posters in backlit frames line each wall, making it feel like an indie movie-plex. I've always loved hanging out down here when I'm not on a mission to salvage the final crumbs of my self-respect.

"Oh! Fab!" Mel exclaims. "I thought you were dragging me down here for some popcorn," she deadpans.

My stomach growls, but I ignore it. We haven't eaten since Mom made us turkey sandwiches for lunch. But crab legs will have to wait. When we get to the bunk room, I stop short, and Mel bumps into my back, which knocks me against the door.

"Whoa!" I whisper-shout, rubbing between my eyebrows.

"Sorry," she says. "I thought we were actually going *into* the room." She gestures to the door handle that I'm currently grasping.

I pause. "What if someone's in there?" I ask, suddenly feeling like this could be an even worse idea than texting Patrick in the first place.

"Who could possibly be in this room?" she asks. "We left Patrick and Bekah and everybody else outside."

She's right, I figure. So, after a deep breath, I turn the doorknob, and we both tiptoe into the dark space. The bunk room is cozy but spacious, with four full beds that are stacked in pairs and built into the walls on either side of the room. At the rear of the room, floor-to-ceiling windows face the back deck, which leads out to the boating dock and the lake. By now, the sun has set, and with the curtains almost fully drawn, only a small lamp on the desk at the window provides a soft glow to the space.

Looking around the room, I spot one unmade bed. In a rush, Mel and I cross over to search for Patrick's phone.

Each bunk has its own nook for storage and a mounted reading light. And to our great luck, when we reach the edge of the unmade bed, we find a phone that looks just like Patrick's plugged into the outlet and resting on the ledge.

Mel crawls across the mattress and pulls the phone off its charger. She presses the power button to wake up the home screen, and sure enough, there's a background image of the Dodgers winning the World Series. We've got the right phone. But when Mel attempts to swipe it open, a black lock screen comes into view.

"You gotta be kidding me. A passcode!" I sigh in defeat, then start to spiral. "What does everyone have to hide these days? What, does he have a criminal past? A secret family? It's like I never knew the kid! Ugh! Whyyy didn't we think of this?"

"Well," Mel says flatly, "it's not like we're professionals."

But we don't have time to despair, because in the next moment, a series of sounds causes us to nearly jump out of our skin—a sharp *click*, a rustle of movement, and the gruff clearing of a throat.

Then a disembodied deep voice creeps across the room. "If you wanted to hide out and drink, all you had to do was ask."

CHAPTER FOUR

FIVE MINUTES EARLIER

If people-watching were an Olympic sport, I'm pretty sure I'd have a gold medal by now. I'm an expert fly on the wall—I'd choose sitting back and watching two people argue over being a part of small talk any day. Unfortunately, I think it's the reason I just got dumped.

Chloe: ur always so in ur head, Tommy

Chloe: it's hard to be around that sometimes

Those were the two texts that popped up on my phone one night after we went out with her friends. Sure, I was quiet a lot of that night. We were at a hibachi restaurant, and I figured it was better to keep my mouth shut than tell her friend

Candice she'd made, like, four microaggressions against me *and* the chef. It was her birthday, after all.

But it's Chloe's last text, the one she sent after I asked if she'd consider giving me a second chance, that I can't stop thinking about.

Yeah. She hit me with a Maya Angelou quote. And there's really nothing you can say back to that. But accepting her closed door doesn't make the pang in my chest go away.

Chloe and I met last fall in our AP English class. On the first day, she came rushing in, almost late, and took the empty seat next to me. She had the bluest eyes I'd ever seen and was dressed in bright colors. But the first thing I noticed was her laugh as she burst through the door with her friend Emma. How she threw her whole body into it—head back, mouth wide open, eyes scrunched closed like she'd just been told the funniest joke on earth. Instantly I wanted to be the one to make her laugh like that.

When that laugh, which seemed to last a whole minute, was over and she opened her eyes, our gazes latched, and she caught me staring. I was surprised when she smiled. And like a mirror, I smiled back. We went out for ramen that night and have been together ever since. Well, up until two weeks ago, when she hit me with what might as well have been a sledgehammer by telling me she would not, in fact, be coming up to spend the summer at my family's lake house. And not because she had other plans. Because she was breaking up with me.

So, during my mom's annual summer bash, I'm holed up down here in the bunk room—the one I was supposed to be sharing with my brother because both of our girlfriends were going to be taking over our rooms upstairs. Now I'm just down here because my upstairs room is being turned into a "craft room" for our mom. I pull back the curtain to get a glimpse out the window of Patrick and our friends and observe what it's like to be "easy to be around." Maybe I should take some notes.

I'm about to save the newest draft of the manuscript I've been fiddling with and shut my laptop when a loud *thud* at the door makes me jump. I groan. If Patrick brought Bekah down here to hook up during the party, I do *not* want to deal with that awkwardness. I talk to my brother about girls, sure. But I don't need to *see* him in action. As the doorknob starts to turn, I dive for the nearest bunk—figuring I'll find a way to sneak out while they're too "busy" to notice. I can just pretend I heard and saw nothing.

But then I hear, "You gotta be kidding me."

I can barely make out the soft whispering from where I'm hiding in the farthest bunk by the window. It takes me a minute, but I recognize the voice. It's Andie, our neighbor and my little brother's old crush. Like me, she's a bit of a quiet one. Her best friend, Mel, is the bigger personality. And that's probably why I've always been a little curious to see Andie come out of her shell. But if you ask Patrick, *unlike* me, Andie's not hard to be around—even if she's probably still mad at me for losing track of my dog on the beach last year. I can't really blame her if she's still pissed. That fish Maisy proudly plopped onto her lap was gnarly.

But none of that explains what she's doing in this room.

There's more movement, a few mumbles, and a deep exhale of disappointment. Then I hear, "It's not like we're professionals" in a dry, sarcastic tone. And that would definitely be Mel.

At this point, I figure I'd rather bust these two for whatever weird thing they've got going on than keep hiding in my own house. So, I quietly crawl out of the bunk to stand. Then I softly clear my throat. "If you wanted to hide out and drink, all you had to do was ask."

As expected, they both jump and scream. Then, out of left field, something small and blunt hits me directly in my chest. I yelp in response, but with my baseball reflexes, I catch the object before it falls to the floor.

"Oh my God!" Mel squelches. "Tommy!"

"Yeah," I respond, catching my breath from the sudden rush of adrenaline. I take a second to inspect the projectile that hit me and realize it's my brother's phone. Now I'm even more intrigued. "It's me, Tommy. You know, in *my* house, where I belong. Which begs the question . . ." I leave the rest of the sentence hanging in the air while I shine the phone's flashlight their way. It's kind of fun treating them like bandits.

"I—I can explain!" Andie finally speaks, palms up like she's being arrested. This time, the typical soft lilt to her voice has a slight edge to it. Her big hazel eyes are bright and wide. Her face is turning red. Glancing down at her short denim skirt and heels, I notice that the outfit she's wearing is not the usual for her—probably Mel's doing. Still, I'm not complaining. Naturally she's on the defensive. And I'm wondering if those wheels in her mind are conjuring up an excuse, or if she's just going to come clean.

"Okay, honestly . . . ," she starts, eyes wild in the bright light. "I was hoping to rekindle things with your brother this summer after what happened on the beach last year . . . which I'm sure you'll remember since it was *your* dog and *her* dead fish that killed the vibe. Anyway . . . so I sent Patrick a . . . let's just call it 'suggestive' . . . text message this morning before I knew he had a girlfriend, and I dragged Mel down here with me because I was hoping to break into his phone to delete it before he had a chance to see it. Apparently he and Bekah have been 'busy' all day and he's been ignoring me, and also she's calling him 'Patty' now?" She pauses to breathe. A relief, since I don't know how she lasted that long. I don't interrupt either, because this is just too good. "Anyway . . . as Mel pointed out, we are clearly amateurs, and didn't think about the fact that obviously your brother's phone would have a passcode, so . . . here we are . . . "

Andie's panting now, hands still frozen in the air, dark curls puffing out around her shoulders. In the light, I zero in on the constellation of freckles that dot her nose and cheeks.

"Wow," is all I can manage to say. Even if I wasn't already the *mostly* silent type, I'd probably have a hard time figuring out what to say after that. Observing people is what I do, and in all my observations, I've noticed that nine times out of ten, people will hide more than they show. But Andie's put all her cards on the table.

As Patrick's brother, I should probably object to the violation of his privacy. But that's not what's happening here. I turn off the flashlight.

"Okay, she confessed," Mel says, very matter-of-fact. "So, what are you gonna do, man? Rat us out? Or can we pretend this all just never happened? Maybe sneak off with the good stuff you mentioned before? Eh?"

"Or," I say, raising my eyebrows, "I could just . . . give you the passcode?" Honestly, it's the least I can do after last year's mishap, which clearly has not been forgotten.

Under the soft glow of the lamplight, I see Andie's full mouth fall open. "You'd do that?" she asks, eyes sparking with disbelief.

"I always thought you were the cool brother," Mel says,

and she's so good, I *almost* believe her. Then she squints at me. "But what's the catch?"

I surprise myself with what I say next. But I've been moping around this house for three days, fiddling with my broken manuscript and lugging around a broken heart. This is—depressingly—the most interesting thing that's happened to me in weeks. "I'm gonna need to see that text."

"Ugh," Andie grunts. "Fine! But you are sworn to secrecy!"

I give her a quick salute and then toss her Patrick's phone. This way, I'll have plausible deniability if he ever asks if *I've* broken into it. "The passcode is one, two, three, four, five, six."

"You're joking," Mel says, stone-faced.

Andie's fingers fly across the screen. "He's not." She holds up the unlocked phone.

"Now you're in," I say. "So, what was so bad that it had you on the verge of committing a crime tonight?"

Shoulders slumped, Andie tosses the phone back to me. And when I look down at the text message she sent my brother, I can only hope my internal reaction can't be read on my face. Then a strange feeling takes ahold of me—like a tightness in my chest. My face heats. It's not secondhand embarrassment. It's more like a strong feeling that I want to make this go away for Andie.

Before I even realize it, I'm deleting the two texts. I toss the phone back. "There you go," I tell her. "All gone. And . . . your secret's safe with me."

She glances down at the phone, then up at me. Her eyes soften and the corners of her mouth curve upward. "Thank you," she says.

Honestly, I would have opened the phone for them without bargaining for it. And now I even feel *kind* of guilty for making Andie show me the text. Because I recognize the look on her face right now as she stands here not quite sure what to do with herself. I heard the signs of it in her voice during her rant too. I know it because I'm right where she is.

Heartbroken.

"Welp, it looks like our business here is done," Mel says, interrupting my thoughts. "Promise we won't breathe a word of this to anyone outside this bunk room?"

Andie nods, and I extend a hand to her. "What happens in the bunk room stays in the bunk room."

We shake on it before the girls turn to leave. And after the door clicks shut, it hits me that this was the first time I've touched Andie Weaver.

CHAPTER FIVE

Me: Did you slip and fall in the bathroom . . . do I need to send a search party?

Mom: No. But close. Hair's just not hair-ing tonight. And my dress is too tight.

Mom: Honey . . . I think I'm gonna skip. Don't be mad. Ok?

Me: Im not mad. But what should I tell ppl?

Me: Mason's dad just asked about you

Me: AGAIN!

Mom: That man won't quit! 😠

Mom: Tell him I'm dead.

Me: Not. Funny.

Mom: I know. Sorry. Tell everybody I have food poisoning?

Mom: And remember, bending the truth is only ok if your mother puts you up to it. 😇

Me: I got you mama. Always.

Mom: Love you, Andie-Bug. ♥

Me: Love you back. ♥

"Mom's not coming," I tell Mel, who's currently having an indecently intimate moment with a crab leg on the other side of our shared hammock.

I sigh while throwing my head back to rest on the woven fabric of the hammock. It's the first time since I walked into this party that I feel like I can relax. Sure, the love of my relatively brief life is officially off the market. But I'm also off the hook. As far as he knows, I'm totally over him—not at all quietly contemplating if I've potentially ruined my chances at happiness forever. Suddenly I'm not feeling so relaxed anymore.

"We gotta help that woman get her spark back," she says between slurps, drawing me out of my downward spiral.

At Mel's mention of a spark, I get a flash of the run-in Mom and I had this morning. "You should have seen her at the general when we ran into Mason's dad. She basically glitched."

Simon Rodriguez, for the past six years, has just been another lake dad to me. He's tall, with the kind of muscles you get from being a carpenter, and he and my mom went to high school together. Sometimes Mom and Dad would allude to the fact that she and Simon didn't get along back in the day and make light of it. And Mom would just make herself scarce whenever all the lake parents hung out.

But over the past year especially, anytime his name comes up, Mom's spine goes straight. Today, when we stopped for the essentials like toilet paper, tampons, chocolate-covered almonds—the works—Simon came down our aisle, and you'd have thought Mom saw a life-size Labubu, by the way she froze and darted the other way, leaving me to say hi and awkwardly wave for both of us.

"Maybe they're in luuuurve," Mel says, her eyes flashing bright.

I roll mine. "I *highly* doubt it," I say, looking up at the stars, like tiny pinpricks in a black sheet of sky. "My mom would rather cut her grass with a pair of toenail clippers than spend two seconds alone with Simon Rodriguez. Pretty sure they were, like, sworn enemies or something back in high school."

"Wait a minute!" Mel blurts out before leaning forward, almost tipping us over onto the grass. Mel rocks backward to steady us. "Maybe this could be our new mission for the summer! I mean, on top of stealing Patrick away from Bekah, of course," she says, and I wonder when we decided that this was part of the plan. I don't have time to ask because she keeps talking. "Enemies-to-lovers *is* my favorite trope," she says with a wink. "You know this."

I love Mel. If she needed a kidney tomorrow, I'd give her mine. But she has a way of doing the Most with poor planning, and I fear trying to set up my newly divorced mom with my dad's friend, no less, is a prime example. Still, I can't pretend the curiosity isn't eating me up inside.

"Let's pump the brakes a sec, 'kay?" I ask. "Mom avoids that man almost as much as she avoids doing taxes and wearing pantyhose. This *is* the guy who—" I don't get to finish my thought because, I realize, she never quite explained what she disliked so much about Simon Rodriguez. Also, Mel's phone starts to vibrate and her face lights up like a candle. I know there's only one person it can be.

"Augie!" she practically shrieks once the video call connects. "Oh my God, babe! Where are you? Are you close? I need you here, like, yesterday."

And that's my cue to get the heck out of this hammock. Which is easier in theory than in practice. Because our legs are tangled in the middle and there's simply no way I'm making a graceful exit. Twenty seconds later, with no help at all from Mel, and after flashing her with my entire underworld—not that she noticed on account of being in full-on flirtation mode with her boyfriend—I'm free of the contraption.

Since Mom flaked on me and Mel's preoccupied, I might as well make a solid attempt at socializing. And even though I'd rather tap-dance barefoot on hot stones than make small talk in front of the last boy I kissed and his new girlfriend,

I've got all summer ahead of me to deal with this awkwardness, so I might as well dive right in.

I take a deep breath and start to snake my way through the crush of cotton sundresses, Hawaiian shirts, linen button-ups, and polos with my eyes peeled for a group of six to eight seventeen-year-olds. To an outsider, our summer crew might look a little bit mismatched. Between us we've got jocks, theater kids, and a mathlete, and Selina even spent one summer leaning into the Goth aesthetic until she discovered that thick black eyeliner, sunscreen, and sweat were not a great combination. But spending every summer and winter together in the mountains from the time you're prepubescent to the time you're just about ready to launch into adulthood does something to bond a group—for better or worse.

When I round the corner on the L-shaped lower deck, I spot our crew all huddled in Adirondack chairs around the fire pit. I reach into my pocket, grab my phone, and snap a photo. It's dark now, so I have to adjust the settings to get the lighting right. But when I do, the glow from the fire casts the perfect wash over everyone, and zooming in, I can see Selina and Mason laughing, Evan whispering something into Rosie's ear as she smiles, and then—at the edge of the frame—Bekah and Patrick . . . *my* Patrick. Only, now he's very obviously hers. Because he's kissing her on the forehead like no one's watching. Except I'm watching. Like a desperate loser lurking in the shadows.

Okay, so we're *not* socializing after all. I can't walk into the metaphorical lion's den of heartbreak and rejection.

Panicked, I swipe out of the photo and stuff my phone back into my pocket. Then I look around for an escape route. I could leave. But not without Mel. *Never leave your girl at a party when you came together* is Best Friend Code 101. I'm about to make a run for more seafood—figuring stuffing my face is a decent alternative—when I'm busted.

"There she is! Andie, over here!" Selina's just spotted me over the flames of the fire pit. I hope she didn't notice me staring at Patrick and Bekah's cuddle session. A girl can only take so much embarrassment in one evening. "Get over here, we're about to play beer pong!"

I guess the crab legs will have to wait.

CHAPTER SIX

TOMMY

My mom really knows how to throw a party. By the time I make it down the hall and into the game room, Andie and Mel have disappeared into the mix of people dancing, laughing, and crowded around the dartboard and pool table. This year, we've probably set the record for highest attendance for a Ling family Summer Kickoff party. And that just makes my game plan of lying low even harder.

"Tommy, there you are!" My dad's voice shoots my way from the direction of the bar. I turn and walk toward him and a man I've never seen. "You gotta meet Rick," Dad says. "This guy was an ace back in our days at USC. I told him not to hold the fact against you that you've defied your old man and are set to become a Bruin in the fall."

I paste on a smile for my dad and stretch out my hand to greet his old teammate. "Nice to meet you, sir." My throat feels scratchy, but I hope that came out sounding more self-assured than I feel.

Rick pumps my hand hard, like he's testing my strength. "Your dad tells me you're an absolute rocket out there on the mound," he says, voice husky and thick—like he's had his fair share of dip and cigarettes. But somehow, like my dad, he's still got a million-dollar smile. I look down and notice they've both got cold beers clutched in their fists.

Dad throws an arm around my shoulder and leans down toward my ear. "So, listen, Tommy," he says. "Rick here's a scout for a minor team out of Rancho Cucamonga, the single-A affiliate for the Dodgers. Tells me he's impressed with your film. Isn't that right, Rick?"

Rick clears his throat. "What I said was, the kid has potential," he clarifies. "But it's true that we're looking to expand this season." He reaches into his pocket and withdraws a crisp white business card. "Give me a call if you want to talk about the future, young man." Then he turns to my dad. "Now, if you gentlemen don't mind, I think I'm gonna go get some of that crab boil."

Dad and Rick tap beers, and the scout walks off. Then

Dad turns to me, and whatever look he sees on my face wipes the grin clean off his.

"Now, don't look at me like that, Tommy," he says, frowning. "We've talked about this a hundred times. Mom and I just want you to have *options*. There's always going to be time for you to write 'the next great American novel.'" He says this part with finger quotes. "But you can't say the same when it comes to baseball. You're in your prime, kid."

The way my dad talks about my writing never fails to make my face prick with heat—like anger and embarrassment are competing to have a go at me. This is a sports family. I've known it since I could walk and talk—which is right around the time I got my first baseball glove. But ever since I could write a sentence, I've known that I wanted to write stories. And when I read *Artemis Fowl* in eighth grade, I got the itch to make a fantasy/sci-fi world of my own.

The truth is, I love both. Baseball was the best thing about high school for me. Not because it made me popular—it didn't. Or scored me points with girls—which in some ways it did. But because it was the one thing that got me out of my head. I surprised myself when I realized that I actually *want* to go to college. And not just to play ball at an elite level but because I want to study creative writing and try my hand at putting shape and form to all my story ideas.

What my dad doesn't seem to realize is that when you already know what you want to do with the next phase of your life, having "options" feels more like a distraction than free-dom. "Dad, you know Patrick's interested in going pro out of high school. Maybe *he* should have Rick's card."

At my suggestion Dad sucks his teeth and scans the room. Then, eyes hard on mine, he leans down to whisper, "I sent him both of your tapes, son. He wanted to talk to *you*."

And with that, Dad pats me on the shoulder and turns back to the party.

Dad probably left me standing at the bar ten minutes ago. And I've spent all of those minutes stuck on the last thing he said. Since we were first able to toss and catch, Patrick and I have been pitted against each other by our dad and even some coaches. "Healthy competition" is what they'd call it. Iron sharpening iron or whatever. And even though my stats have always had the slight edge on his, Patrick's been the one with all the heart and drive. It's what I admire most about my brother. So the scout eyeing *me* and not him when I don't even know if I want to go pro really doesn't seem fair.

Now I feel like I need air—and space. Lucky for me, just outside the sliding glass door and past a crowd of about forty people on the deck is exactly the perfect place for me to get both. The end of our boating dock. I dip behind the bar and grab a cold root beer and head outside. But after just two steps into the crisp night air—"Tommy!"

I cringe at the sound of my name. It's Patrick. "Dude,

where have you been? Tell me you haven't been at your desk working on that book."

I shrug and am about to say *See ya later* when he grabs my wrist to tug me closer.

"Hey, Mom said Dad brought a scout for the minors to the party. D'you meet him yet?" he asks, his voice hushed but excited.

Rubbing the back of my neck, I shrug again. "We talked for maybe half a minute inside with Dad," I say, trying to play it cool. "Nothing major." I know it's my brother's biggest dream to go pro, and his second-biggest dream to see *me* go pro first. Years ago, when we were kids, it was mine too. But things change.

"Well?" he urges, eyes going wide. Bekah wraps an arm around his waist, listening in. "You gotta give me more than that, bro. Is there gonna be a meeting?"

"He gave me his card," I tell him. "I'll call him next week, I guess." I'm hoping this will satisfy Patrick's curiosity at least for tonight. But the truth is, I haven't decided what I'm going to do with the card that's practically burning a hole in my pocket.

"My big bro!" Patrick says, smacking me on the butt. And now I'm wondering how much of that secret booze stash I told the girls about he's partaken of tonight. "It's really about to happen for you, man."

By now, we've reached the gazebo near the tree line of

our backyard, where the rest of our group is setting up for a game of beer pong. It's a safe distance away from the main party and any parental units who'd object.

"You guys hear the news?" Pat shouts as we climb the steps. He claps me on the back and announces, "My big bro has a meeting with a scout!"

Loud hoots sound out from around the folding table. String lights hang with the vines overhead, so it's bright enough for us to see the game even long after the sun's gone down. I can see the lake shimmering through the trees behind us, and right about now, I'm wishing I could jump into it.

"Just make sure you don't forget about us," Mason calls out. "You know, the little people."

I wave him off. "How could I forget the guy who's owed me a hundred bucks for three years and never paid up?" I shoot back.

"Well, tonight's your chance to get it back," Mel cuts in. "All right, we need teams!"

And I'm relieved because she's just given me the perfect opportunity to slip away without anyone noticing. They'll all be too busy pairing up for beer pong. I take a sly step toward the dock, but Augie, Mel's boyfriend, yells, "Not so fast, slugger!" He claps me on the shoulder and drags me backward. "Andie needs a partner." He points over to a wide-eyed, red-faced Andie.

She's shaking her head. "Noooope! No! It's fine. I'm not

playing. I'm just gonna go . . . over there." She insists, pointing to nowhere in particular, before attempting to *also* escape down the steps.

When Mel catches hold of Andie's wrist, they start whispering in uppercase letters with broad hand gestures. Evan, whose girlfriend, Selina, is busy carefully lining up the Solo cups, slinks over to me, with beer and nachos on his breath. "Dude. You gotta put an end to this. It's gonna kill the vibe."

Before I can ask him who dropped maintaining "the vibe" onto *my* shoulders, Andie's stomping over to us with her brow furrowed and her arms crossed like a toddler who was given five minutes in a far corner. Her eyes are hard on mine, and it feels kind of strange to be around her now, after our encounter in the bunk room—like we've got a little secret. Because, technically, we do. And the fact that I'm one of only two people here who know just how much she's still into my brother, the other one being Mel, means I'm probably best equipped to help her out right now.

"Tell me you're good at this, Tommy," she says, her eyes hard on mine. "Because beer makes me sick." And it almost sounds like a threat.

For a split second, I have a flashback of Andie dry-heaving on the beach. I'm good at beer pong, but so is Patrick. So our best chance of getting out of this with Andie intact is gonna be for me to take her swigs for her.

Fifteen minutes later, Patrick's just sunk another Ping-

Pong ball into one of our cups. And like I've done the last three turns, I prepare to fall on the sword, because I'm both chivalrous *and* squeamish at the sight of puke.

"Tommy, you can't keep taking Andie's cups for her!" Bekah shouts from across the table like a little narc. "It's cheating."

I'm about to protest and say it's not that big a deal, when Mel cuts in, shooting daggers with her eyes. "Lighten up, Becky. This isn't the World Cup."

Probably to ease the tension, with a self-sacrificing groan Andie pushes me aside and presses up to the edge of the table.

I lean down to whisper, practically beg, into her ear, "Andie, you *really* don't have to do this."

But she's too busy staring Bekah down like she's her evil shadow to hear me. And before anyone can stop her, Andie swipes the red Solo cup and throws it back, downing it all in a gulp so big, we can hear it.

"She's gonna regret that," Mel murmurs to my left.

To my right, Andie lurches. Luckily, nothing comes up . . . yet.

"Pretty sure we all are," Augie says next.

Mel runs for the beer bucket and dumps it. She then places it under Andie's face just in time for the regurgitated beer to splash-land inside.

"All right. I think we're done here," I shout. "This was so

much fun, Patrick and Bekah. You win," I say flatly.

Patrick looks about as happy as if I told him he won a rubber chicken. Bekah's beaming and wrapping her arms around his waist. And for a split second, I'm thinking about the last time Chloe hugged me like that. But Andie's coughing again, so I should probably go find her some water.

Mason and Olivia are already resetting and filling the Solo cups for round two. Mel's holding back Andie's hair, and I'm heading inside for that water and a washcloth. On my way, I'm shaking my head, fully aware that *this* is the peer pressure our parents warned us about.

CHAPTER SEVEN

TOMMY

"A penny for your thoughts?"

The sound of a soft voice approaching from behind makes me jump and almost chuck my root beer into the lake. For someone as observant as me, it's a surprise I never noticed her footsteps on the dock. Was probably too lost in my thoughts. Or maybe it was the sound of King Harvest's "Dancing in the Moonlight" wafting over the sound system.

But I know the voice. I'm surprised to hear it too, since I was sure she'd gone home after the beer pong debacle.

Turning, I find Andie walking toward me on the dock.

Her denim skirt is almost completely hidden by an oversize hoodie, and her long curls blow wild in the draft from the lake. I clear my throat and ask, "What are you, a grandma trapped in a seventeen-year-old's body?"

She laughs, kneeling to sit by me on the dock. "No, but my grandma *did* always ask me that question whenever she found me off somewhere alone staring deep into space," she says. "At some point, I realized I gave her a lot of my thoughts but never did get any of those pennies."

Everything that's happened since Andie and Mel broke into the bunk room has thrown me for a loop. The text. The scout. The fact that one swig of beer could make a person lose *that* much of their daily nutrients. And now Andie has voluntarily come out to join me on the dock when I don't think we've *ever* been alone together. Instead of overthinking it, I decide I might as well just go with it. "Scammed by your very own flesh and blood," I say after missing a beat or two. "Has to hurt."

"Yeah." She sighs. "I got her back, though. One time I hid her bifocals in the yarn bin of her craft closet, and it took her almost an entire week to find them."

The gulp of root beer I just took spews out of my mouth and into the lake below our dangling feet, propelled by the laugh that bursts out of my chest.

Andie gasps. "Kidding! Oh my God, I would never," she shouts, between heaps of laughter. "I know we're not exactly besties, Tommy, but do you really think I'm capable of elder abuse?"

"Well, I didn't think you were capable of phone hacking until a couple hours ago. But here we are. I don't know what to believe anymore," I say, teasing her back, surprised at how easy the flow of our conversation feels. "Where's your side-kick, by the way?"

At my question, Andie's face falls the tiniest bit. If I hadn't been studying her expression since the moment she joined me on the dock, I probably would have missed it. "Likely somewhere rounding the bases with Augie, and I refuse to be a bystander to all of that . . ." She makes an exaggerated face, like she just swallowed something sour.

"Let me guess . . . you're not a fan of PDA, huh?" I ask her.

For a long moment, she's completely quiet. I don't know if I've asked the wrong thing or if she's just carefully considering her answer.

"No, it's not that. It's just—" She pauses again, turning back to the patio. I track her line of sight until my eyes land on where my brother and Bekah are cuddled up in the same Adirondack chair by the fire pit. And suddenly it all makes sense. A pang of guilt rises in my stomach.

"I'm sorry, you know," I tell her, turning back to look at her profile now. A spray of dark freckles covers her nose and cheeks. I'm thinking about the fact that I've never seen her try to cover them up with makeup, when she distracts me by catching my stare. She looks confused, and I remember I've just apologized without explaining myself. "About last summer, with Maisy and the fish," I rush to explain. Her mouth opens, then shuts, and her cheeks flush. "I feel like if that didn't happen . . ." Now it's my turn to trail off.

"It would be *me* up there with Patrick right now?" she asks, turning back to the patio, where my brother's got Bekah on his lap, rubbing her nose with his, like some sappy cartoon. Everyone's laughing at a story Mason's in the middle of. They've all got marshmallows loaded up on sticks by the fire. They're fully in the mix of things, and here I am with Andie . . . two sad sacks on the outskirts. "Where is Maisy, by the way? Shouldn't she be around here snooping for table scraps or lovingly slobbering on the guests?"

This makes me laugh. The old girl's become a bit of a mascot for our lake crew. And knowing I won't have her or Chloe to hang out with up here this summer has been a major letdown. "She's back in Santa Barbara with our grandparents," I explain. "Vet said the mountains aren't great for her lungs at her age."

Andie's shoulders slump. "I'm sorry, Tommy," she says while placing her hand on my forearm. Her palm is warm and soft, and when I look down at where she's touching me, she pulls away, stuffing both hands under her thighs. "Contrary to popular belief," she says, "I think Maisy's a great dog. Even if she is a troublemaker."

For a second, I forgot we'd been talking about Andie and Patrick. "I guess I always kind of assumed you and my brother would give things a try someday. I think we all did," I admit.

Andie gasps, and it draws me back to the moment. "You felt guilty!" she says. "And that's why you did what you did for me back in the bunk room. It all makes sense! If you hadn't let go of the leash, it could be me on Patrick's lap right now, running my fingers through his hair and cackling at whatever lame joke Mason's subjecting them all to."

"Okay, well, we don't know that for sure," I say in my defense. Even if I'm not willing to say it out loud, I do feel guilty. But she might be reaching a little with the rest. When I hesitate, Andie glares at me. "I'm just saying. Any number of factors could have prevented you and Patrick from getting together over the past year."

"Is that right?" she asks, chin stuck forward, all smug. "So, you, Maisy, and the fish had *nothing* to do with it?"

Cornered now, I stumble over my thoughts—my words, too. "Let's just say I feel your pain. I . . . I empathize," I tell her, my eyes darting back at the water.

"Hmm," she says. "I sense a story here." She studies me, drumming her fingers on the dock, looking like she's trying to piece a mystery together. "You were in that room alone, in the dark, while everyone else was out here enjoying the party."

I just continue to study the ripples of the water under the moonlight, feeling her gaze on my face.

"You weren't just doing your typical antisocial Tommy bit. You were . . . you were in there moping!"

I still don't meet her eyes.

"Earlier, Mel said something about *your* girlfriend coming up this summer too. Wait . . ." She stops, and I can *feel* rather than see her eyes grow intense on my profile. The heat of her stare almost singes me. "She's not here, is she?"

"I don't have a girlfriend," I grind out, and I finally turn and meet her eyes. In the span of a second, the light in hers changes from delightful curiosity to intense recognition. She looks back at our group of friends surrounding the fire pit. Then she turns back to me. No words pass between us, but a mutual understanding does. We are in this heartbreak together.

CHAPTER EIGHT

"She dumped me," Tommy says. His words come out bluntly, but I can tell that the wound is fresh. He clears his throat and turns back to the water. I'm starting to think looking at the lake feels safer than looking at me.

"Oh," is all I can say. And now I feel horrible for forcing this confession. "That. Sucks." Suddenly I'm not so good with words either. "I mean, look. Her loss, right?" I say to lighten things up a bit.

He laughs. But nothing feels all that funny right now. Except for the fact that the two of us—I don't even think I'd call us friends. Acquaintances? The two of us acquaintances have something in common. We're both in love with people who clearly are *not* in love with us. And we're stuck in the mountains for weeks with nothing to do but obsess over how pathetic we are, while all of our friends are coupled up. I'll get to see what I could have had but can't anymore, right in front of my eyes every day. And Tommy gets to feel the absence of what he had and lost too.

I don't know what's worse.

"I have an idea," I say. I'm not sure where any of this is coming from or where it's going, but I just open my mouth and let it flow. "Let's not be heartbroken losers this summer."

A sharp huff of laughter bursts out of Tommy. "Ummm, okay," he says. "Care to elaborate?"

"I mean, let's not just sit and let the summer *happen* to us. Let's not be bystanders," I explain, pausing to build the plane as I fly—I'm totally winging this. "What if you and I stick together this summer? Team up, like in beer pong?"

Now he turns to me, one thick eyebrow raised. But not in a *What are you talking about, you lunatic?* kind of way. But more so in an *Okay . . . I'm listening* kind of way. I clear my throat and take the dive.

"What if, whenever you're feeling like a loser because of your . . ." I trail off, waving my hand in his general direction, searching for the right words. I give up and land on "*Situation . . .* instead of turning to your typical silent brooding, you call or text me something like *SOS*, and I can come and save you from yourself?"

Tommy doesn't say anything. He just simply stares at me like he wants me to keep talking. So I do. "*And* in return, whenever I can't stomach watching Patty and Becky in all their glory and I feel like I'm going to implode from the tragedy of my own depressing lack of a love life"—I pause to take a breath—"I text you, and you come running to make sure I don't walk into the lake?"

Long seconds go by without a word from Tommy. I'm on the verge of retracting the entire arrangement when he finally shows signs of life. Surprising me, he laughs. His laugh gets bigger and bigger, flashing me with a perfect row of pearly white teeth that shine under the moonlight. And suddenly I start to feel like a complete idiot.

"This was dumb," I mumble, pulling my feet up from the edge of the dock. "You obviously do fine all on your own." I'm getting up to leave when his hand grasps my forearm. His palm feels a little rough but warm.

"Wait," he says. His voice is soft but insistent. And his eyes—there's nothing funny about the look he's giving me now. "Stay. I'm sorry. I wasn't laughing *at* you, Andie. Please stay, and I'll explain."

I settle back in next to him, crossing my arms over my chest. It's not every day I go around propositioning people. And I've never been one to take rejection on the chin. But today, I'm 0 for 2 and seconds away from a meltdown.

For a split second, Tommy eyes me warily—like he's wondering if I'll push him into the lake. I wave my hands for him to get on with it, so he sucks in a long breath, and on the exhale, he spills his guts to me.

"So, everybody knows that you and Patrick have been, like . . . close, or whatever you want to call it, for, like, four summers and winters now, right? And I've always been kind of comfortable on my own, for the most part. But this summer was going to be different. I was gonna have *my* person. Patrick was gonna have his. And everything was finally going to feel . . . okay. You know?" Tommy pauses, leaving me to wonder where *I* was going to fit into that scenario. I'm about to ask him exactly that when he launches into part two.

"Except things didn't turn out that way. Obviously," he says. And I don't think I've ever heard Tommy Ling sound *sad* before. Disinterested? Bored? Annoyed? Sure. All of the above. But his green eyes are particularly shiny right now, and I don't think it's just the moonlight reflecting off them. Before I have time to fully process this new side of him, he's talking again.

"And now I'm back to riding solo. I mean, you called it earlier," he says with a self-deprecating chuckle. It shakes off that moment of sadness. "I was literally sitting in the dark with my laptop in the middle of a party. I guess I'd sorta written off the whole summer as this major loss. But here you are, offering to be . . . well, not my person like *that* . . . but my somebody for the summer. And I . . . I don't know . . . After all these years seeing you with Patrick, I just never expected to find *us* here—you and me. You know?"

"To be clear, Tommy, I'm not asking for your hand in marriage," I clarify, smiling now.

Tommy runs a hand over his face and back into his hair, mussing it up. "Wow . . . I just bared my soul to you, Andie Weaver."

"I'm just trying to make sure we're on the same page here," I tell him, slipping out of my wedges to dip my foot into the lake and lightly splash his. "But does all of that mean that you're up for it?"

Another strong exhale from Tommy. Then he extends his hand for me to shake.

"We have a deal," he says. He raises an eyebrow. "On one condition: Let's not just get *through* the summer. Let's . . . try to move on?"

"I'm good with that," I tell him honestly. More than anything else, that's what I want. I don't want to pine and be filled with regret, thinking of what could have been between me and Patrick. And I don't want to root against him and Bekah, either—I'm not tryna be a home-wrecker or anything. I just want to . . . process, heal, and glow up. That's all.

"Okay." He nods, seemingly satisfied. "This summer, you call or text me, I come running."

"Well, no one said you had to *run*," I say. I extend my hand and take a deep lungful of lake air. "But we have a deal?"

Tommy encloses my hand in his. "We have a deal."

"So how was the paaarty?" Mom asks. The end of her sentence gets wrapped up in an epic yawn that lasts longer than I thought was even possible. And before I know it, I'm yawning too. Either Mel was right, and yawns *are* contagious, or I'm exhausted from staying up and replaying every detail of yesterday—from the Text to the Dock—over in my mind until my body finally shut down in an act of protest at four a.m. Now it's eight, and Mom and I are not so patiently waiting for the coffee maker to finish percolating our morning fix.

Before answering her, I stretch and rub my eyes. They're

probably sore from me doomscrolling through my old messages with Patrick. A steady stream of jokes, plans, silly memes, and Spotify playlists that dissolved into the pitiful last words each of us typed out but never acknowledged. His—so that kiss . . . we gonna talk about it? And mine, a whole month later—Hey Patrick! How's school?

Could I *be* more lame?

"Andie-Bug." Mom's voice makes me jump. She's mixing up pancakes by the sink but turns to look over her shoulder. "Did you hear me, sweetie? I wanna hear all about the party!

"It was . . ." I pause, drop my arms, and search for something to call it other than a hot mess. I land on "a surprise."

"Oh?" Mom says, as she pulls two mugs down from the cupboard. Her dark brows wiggle, and a slight smirk pulls across her lips. "Spill the tea!"

Mom sets our mugs on the smooth butcher block between us and rests her elbows on the surface. She folds her hands under her chin, and her excitement is so cute that I bite back the urge to demand that she never ask me to "spill the tea" again.

We settle onto stools on opposite sides of the kitchen island. Mom's face is framed by the window behind the sink, and the early-morning sunlight makes the tight coils of her messy bun glow in a shade of deep golden brown. She's wrapped tight in a fuzzy robe and is wearing the thick-rimmed glasses she only wears in the house. Even though

I'm sure she'd pick her appearance apart into a million tiny pieces, in this moment, she is my favorite version of herself—no makeup, no frills. Just Mom.

"Well, you know how me and Patrick have had these vibes for . . . well, always?" I start, still unsure of how much I want to let her know about all the drama.

I feel like I'm constantly fighting an internal battle between *desperately* wanting her advice and also needing to keep my secrets. Because Veronica Washington-Weaver is a particular brand of mama bear. The kind that makes a personal enemy of those who so much as look at their young the wrong way. Love it. Sure. But it could backfire if all that primal energy was directed at the guy who used to be my closest friend at the lake. I weigh my options and settle on letting her in.

"Ye-eees," Mom says, dragging out the word like she's bracing herself for drama.

"Well . . . I never told you this, but . . ." And then I pause. Because I guess those texts really got to me. Also, it's one thing to vent about guys and disappointment to your best friends. But when it's your mom, it feels more raw. I'm surprised when a single tear falls down my cheek.

Mom's rounding the island in a hurry. "Honey!"

I swipe the tear with my sleeve and clear my throat. "It's okay. I'm fine," I assure her as she rubs my back. "It's just that at the end of last summer, me and Patrick kind of kissed, and then we didn't talk for almost a year?" I'm giving her the CliffsNotes, but she'll get the point.

"Wait . . . so you 'kind of' kissed, or you *kissed* kissed, and then he ghosted you?" she asks, eyebrows drawing together, and I can see the mama bear rearing her feral head.

"It's a long story. But after the kiss, I kind of ghosted him," I tell her. She raises an eyebrow. "I know! I know!" I say, waving a hand to rush past her silent judgment. "It doesn't even matter anymore because now all of a sudden he's popped up with this whole entire girlfriend who's *here* for the summer."

Mom's jaw falls open, creating a perfect O shape of her mouth. "She's staying with the Lings next door?" she asks. "And you met her last night at the party?"

I nod. But I add a dramatic flair by also slumping down to drop my forehead to the island.

Mom reaches over to play with my hair. "Oh, Andie-Bug . . ." She hums. "If I had known, I would have put on a hat, squeezed into that stupid dress, and flung myself across the lawn to . . . I don't know. Be a mom."

"It's fine," I mumble, looking up through a mess of my own dark curls. "I'm fine. Can't keep a baddie down for long."

Mom laughs. "That's my girl. And besides . . ." She brushes the hair out of my eyes so I can see her clearly. "Honey, it's your last summer before senior year. You and Patrick have been like an old question that's gone unanswered for quite some time now. Maybe this is your chance to . . . I don't know, use the summer to ask *new* questions. And try to get the answers this time."

"Hmm," I say. "Deep, Mom. Have you been listening to self-help podcasts again?" She rolls her eyes and smiles while my phone buzzes on the island.

Mel: dont u think I forgot about our mission

Last I checked, we had no plans for deep-space travel, so I type back, ?????

Mel: ur mom + Simon Rodriguez = rebound summer

Mel: DUH

I text back, slow your roll! need more intel first!

Because I'm not convinced just yet that what we've got on our hands is a potential love story instead of a potential disaster. If this is going to work, we've got to do our due diligence. I *just* got comfortable with the concept of my parents falling for people who aren't each other. It helped that Dad's already taken the plunge and gotten himself a girlfriend. My parents were married as long as I've been alive, and though it's been four months since the divorce, Mom's acting like her life's on pause. She hardly socializes. Practically lives in athleisure. And started thrifting like she's auditioning for *American Pickers*. I'm giving her some slack, though, because I've seen enough *Oprah* clips to know that everybody heals at their own pace and in their own way. But I'd like to see my mom come out of this rut sooner rather than later.

And either she's a psychic or Mel and I are predictable

creatures, because she asks, "Does Mel want to come over for pancakes?"

Next she's pouring the long-awaited liquid gold into our two oversize and mismatched coffee mugs—mine a tessellation of chubby cats, hers a graphic one that says *Java Good Day!* One whiff of the darkly sweet Colombian brew has me wiggling my shoulders and questioning if I might have a problem.

I take a sip, and for three seconds, I have no qualms. That's until I look at our two mugs and get a brief flash of the third one that used to be here too. It was enormous. It said *Spill the Beans.* And almost always there were two enormous hands steadying it while Mom poured it full.

Now Dad's mug is shoved somewhere in the back of the cupboard, where it will probably stay until November, when the house belongs to him again. Because as I keep having to remind myself, in the After of us, summers at Big Bear belong to Mom and winters belong to Dad. And while a small, quiet part of me still wonders if the three of us could find our way back together, it seems like that future is not in the cards.

Well, at least Dad has moved on. I can't say the same for Mom. She went on a few increasingly disastrous dates with men from apps and then gave up. Based on her stories, the male species is *not* okay. Dad has had it way easier. He met his girlfriend, Trishell, at a law conference three months after he moved out of our house. I only met her once with Dad over bibimbap in Koreatown. But now they live together, and yesterday he sent me a picture of the ring he plans to propose with—something that's been making me itch for twenty-four hours. Mom has no idea. I take one look at her mouthing *I love you*s into her coffee mug and rub the pang in my chest. Then I pick up my phone and text my friend.

    Me: Come over for pancakes?

    Mel: Be there in 5!

"So, Ms. Veronica, and I'm only asking because Andie's been holding out on me . . . ," Mel says while aiming an accusing glare at me over her stack of steaming pancakes. "What went down between you and Simon Rodriguez in high school to make you hate him so much?"

The sneak attack makes Mom choke on a blueberry and makes me almost stab my tongue with my fork. I shoot laser beams back at Mel with my eyes. But she just sits there, unable or unwilling to read the room. Her eyes remain bright with anticipation for the can of worms she's just popped the lid on.

I turn to Mom, who has managed to dislodge the blueberry from her windpipe. Like Mel, I'm also dying to know the backstory.

Mom coughs a few more times. "Um, Mel, why . . . I mean, what makes you so curious about that?" she asks, her voice raw. Like that blueberry really did some damage. And she's turning a little red in the face.

For a split second, Mel looks kind of unsure. Like just maybe she overstepped. She recovers quickly, though. Shrugging, she says, "Well, Ms. Veronica, it's the lake. People talk."

Mom clears her throat again. "And what do people say—ahem—when they talk?" The words come out slow and determined, almost like she's backing Mel into a corner.

Mel's eyes dart my way, and instead of saving my friend from herself, I let my eyes fall to my coffee mug—wondering for a moment if I can get my summer tan to match the coffee's shade, now that I've added some almond milk creamer. Mel chose this life of danger, not me.

As expected, she decides to abandon ship. "It's okay, Ms. V. You don't have to tell me. A girl's entitled to *some* secrets."

At this, Mom laughs. But it's an uneasy one. I'm relieved that Mel decided to stop pressing.

At the same time, now I'm even more curious to get to the bottom of whatever went down between her and Simon Rodriguez.

CHAPTER TEN

Mom and I arrive at Ski Beach with our sun hats, beach towels, and summer reads, well prepped for a day of sun-rotting with the best of them. Since arriving at the lake, I've been watching her closely. Even more closely than I already was since Dad moved out. And if I thought the spark in her was dull before, these days, it seems like it's almost completely snuffed out.

I think my mom is sad.

Which means there is no way on earth I can tell her about the Ring. At least not until she's got something fun and flirty going on for herself.

"How about that spot over there?" Mom asks, pointing at some open sand by the rock wall. It's close enough for us to get a little shade.

"Perfect!" I reply, and we head over to set up.

Twenty minutes later, Mom's dozed off on her stomach—sunglasses scrunched against her nose, and the murder mystery she DNF'd last week but swore to give another try this morning is already abandoned. I'm five chapters into a new rom-com about dueling DJs when a cackle in the distance steals my attention. I look over and take in a sight I wish I could physically cut out of the memory cortex of my brain.

A few dozen yards away, by Mason's bright green tent, Bekah is straddling Patrick as he lies in the sand. She's got her phone aimed at his face, and she's recording him *singing* to her. For a moment, I picture an airplane flying by with a sky banner that reads GET A ROOM . . . AND VOICE LESSONS.

I flip over to face the other direction and try to focus on the DJs. Ten minutes later, I get a text from Mel: where r u?

Me: at the beach with Mom

Mel: We're here too! Come to Mason's tent!

During Patrick and Bekah's earlier PDA show, I'd have been willing to streak down the beach before going near the tent. But at this point, all my friends are over there, and I'm starting to feel like *not* going to say hi is more of a statement.

I look at my mom. "Mom," I whisper. "I'm just gonna go say hi to Mel and the guys real quick. Be back soon."

By the way she mumbles and turns her head, I'm not sure if she heard me through her nap. But I get up and trudge through the sand over to the tent. When I get there, Evan and Mason are tossing around a football and Selina's French braiding Olivia's wet hair.

"Hey, guys!" I say, hoping my smile hides how nauseous I feel. Because Patrick and Bekah are right here too, basically fused together at the mouth.

"Bestie!" Mel shouts, before climbing off Augie's lap and coming over to give me a hug. "Wanna do a shot?"

"Can't," I tell her, holding back the shudder at the memory of last night's beer pong. Truth is, I've learned that when it comes to drinking, I need to pick a lane and stay there. Sure, while a nice buzz can be fun, hard alcohol and most beers simply aren't for me and my weak constitution. But I settle for the simple truth. "I'm here with my mom."

"Boooooooooo!" everybody shouts at once, and I roll my eyes.

"You probably should take it easy after last night anyway," Augie says, mimicking me puking after beer pong. Mel pretends to swat at him with her sun hat, and he ducks out of the way.

"You feeling okay?" Patrick asks from behind me. I'd turned my back to the happy couple, out of self-preservation, so I'm shocked he was even listening in on our convo.

Spinning, I clear my throat and plaster on a big smile. "I'm great!"

"Beer never really was your thing," he says. And I don't miss the way Bekah's face twitches just slightly. I wonder if she knows about us. That we used to be closer. That we kissed last year at this very lake.

I realize I'm staring, lost in my thoughts, when Mel cups my elbow. "Hey!" she says. "Me and Augie are gonna go get some sun on the rock wall. Wanna come with?"

"Nah," I say. "I should get back to my mom."

I say bye to everyone and head over to where we've set up our towels. Mom's done with her nap now and scrolling on her phone. "Everybody having fun?" she asks. "And being good?"

Laughing, I plop down next to her on my towel. "Something like that," I tell her.

She shakes her head. "You don't have to babysit me, Andie. If you want to hang with your friends, you can," she says. "I *do* have a life, you know. Once Tawny finishes up her nail appointment, we're going antiquing." She's referring to Mel's mom—her summertime bestie and thrifting partner.

I'm happy for Mom that she's finding things to do for her first "single" summer at the lake. But when she's gone, I'll be stuck alone on the beach. I hate how awkward I feel in the friend group now. With everyone coupled up and me on the outs, it's like we all started a game of musical chairs that I lost.

But then I remember Tommy. Our deal. Are we really doing this?

Only one way to find out. I reach into my tote bag, grab my phone, and make my very first call for rescue.

CHAPTER ELEVEN

Out of the Feral Lands—
Draft One

CHAPTER FOUR

Sonam and Maxis stood blindfolded, surrounded by more than one hundred witnesses at the center of the king's court. For them, the space was silent except for the rush of blood that pounded in their ears. And they could feel the wild tread of their hearts galloping in their chests, and the gnawing ache from the chains that gripped their wrists and ankles. Both sensations were as familiar to them as they were unwelcome.

Sonam pictured her mother and Maery, her little sister, behind the straps of hide that were wrapped tight around her head. Without Sonam, who would help soothe Maery's night terrors? Who would take her mother's place when the dark clouds of sadness swooped in, rendering her all but immobile, so that she could no longer perform her elaborate dances for the king's court?

Sonam began to cry. Silent, at first. Fat tears, one after another, leaking from her eyes. But as the faces of her mother and sister grew more vivid in her mind's eye, Sonam could not stifle the sob that bloomed in her chest.

Sonam and Maxis knew they had to be silent. In the Feral Lands, for an Usher to be heard without cause was recognized as a defiant act. And in the presence of the king, unbidden sounds were received as nothing more than

~~a cry for punishment.~~

~~Nothing more than a plea for pain.~~

Type and delete. Type and delete. It's the story of my life these days. I've been stuck trying to finish this chapter since I locked myself in the bunk room during the party.

Out of the Feral Lands has taken a bit of a dark turn these past few weeks. Originally I'd planned a story about two star-crossed outcasts who band together to overtake their oppressive government. Then Chloe broke up with me over text, and now Sonam and Maxis are political prisoners on the verge of being sentenced to fates worse than death. Maybe it's the doom and gloom that's got me in a creative fog. But I'm willing to go down the rabbit hole and see where it takes me in the name of my art.

Bzzzz!

My phone vibrates on the desktop, tearing me away from the manuscript I've been tweaking all morning. When I reach for it, the notification shows a name I never expected to see again: Chloe.

With shaky fingers, I swipe open the text. It's a picture of my baseball cap. I zoom in on the corner of the image to get a closer look at her hand, where she's gripping the brim of my varsity hat. Because I'm pathetic like that. The first glimpse I get of her in weeks, and even though it's just a stack of bracelets on her wrist and her slim fingers with their chipped blue nail polish, I'm still I'm hanging on to every detail. Another text comes through, putting an end to my mental note taking.

Chloe: found this today . . .

I don't know how long I sit staring at that gray bubble of text waiting for something, *anything*, else to come through from her to give me some context. When it's clear that this is all I'm getting, I stretch my fingers and prepare to type a response. Then it hits me that I have no idea what to say. There are a million things I want to ask her. Starting with: Is she dating someone new? And: Does she regret dumping me?

Just as I'm about to type something I'll probably regret later, my mom's voice floats in from the hallway.

"Tommyyy! Why don't you go down to the beach with your brother and Bekah, sweetie?"

Two seconds later, I'm thwacked from behind by a pair of swim trunks. I quickly save the Word document before turning around to give my attacker a piece of my mind—because, well . . . priorities.

"Mom. Come on, I—" Turning to face the hallway, I stop short when I notice Dad standing next to Mom within the doorframe of the bunk room, with a heavily satisfied grin on his face. I should have known he was the one with the perfect aim. I groan internally over the fact that I'm being double-teamed.

I turned eighteen a month ago. Which technically means I'm a grown man who can do what he wants and all that, but I promised my parents I'd give them this one last summer at the lake. After that, I fully intend to fill my breaks with back-packing trips in South America or internships in New York or London. Maybe they're hovering because they know this. And maybe I'm giving in because I know it too.

I clear my throat and decide to bargain with the terrorists. "I'll head down there in a little bit. Just need to finish up this chapter." I turn back to my desk, hoping that will be the end of it, desperately waiting for my return to solitude.

But Dad stalks into the room and closes my laptop with his index finger. "Not so fast, my boy. Patrick and Bekah left an hour ago, and your mother and I are not letting you spend the whole summer holed up in here sulking."

I don't know what's worse, the fact that I got dumped or the fact that everyone in my life knows that I got dumped.

Ping! Another text comes through, and on instinct I glance down to check it.

Chloe: I can mail it to you at the lake

Groaning, externally this time, I rub the back of my neck and briefly imagine disappearing into the dystopian world I've created. Now that it's clear Chloe has no intention of seeing me to return the hat, I'm practically itching to get back to the Feral Lands. To Sonam and Maxis—two teens who belong to an ancient society underclass known as the Ushers. In addition to serving the Heirs, Ushers are forbidden to make love matches. But Sonam and Maxis can't resist the pull that has drawn them together since they were kids. Right now I'm tweaking a pivotal beat in chapter four after their defiance of the Heir King is revealed by a hidden enemy. Sonam and

Maxis get dragged to the king's court, where they await their punishment in front of one hundred witnesses.

The moment is the inciting incident, the kick that gets the ball rolling down the hill for the rest of the story. And Ski Beach is not enticing enough to tear me away from the blinking cursor on my screen or the flood of ideas in my head.

Just when I'm about to make another false promise to my parents to head down to the beach soon, my phone pings again.

Andie: SOS.

Next she drops a pin for her location on the beach. A guilt trip from Mom and Dad might not be enough to tear me away from my laptop, but last night Andie and I made a deal.

I pick up my swim trunks from where they fell onto the ground and stand. Making a show of sliding down my basketball shorts to reveal the boxers I have on underneath, I say, "Can I at least get some privacy?" Mom gasps and laughs and covers her eyes. Then, satisfied at their success, my parents leave me alone to get changed.

Ski Beach is bright and hot in the early afternoon. The rippling blue lake shines blinding white in the places where the sun reflects off it. With Afrobeats blasting in my earbuds, I walk the half mile or so from our lake house down to the shore carrying a paddleboard, my towel, and a small cooler of drinks and snacks. I figured I shouldn't arrive empty-handed to my first assignment as Andie's rescuer. Even popped into our pantry to dip into my mom's dried-mango stash, since I saw Andie practically inhaling it at the party.

As I get closer to the water, I spot Evan and Mason's signature highlighter-green tent. I shut off my earbuds and hear music from a nearby speaker.

Mason cups his hands around his mouth and calls out, "Aye! So the other Ling bro finally decided to joins us!"

"Had to let you get the beach warmed up for me!" I shout back. When I get to the tent, we clasp hands and pat each other on the back before Bekah trots over to give me a side hug.

Patrick's a few paces behind her. They're both wet and slightly winded, like they've just come up from paddling in the lake.

"Mom and Dad finally got you away from that laptop, huh?" my brother says with a firm clap on my shoulder.

I swallow down the knot of embarrassment that starts to rise in my throat. I don't hide my writing on purpose or anything like that. But I've learned over the years that the one thing I actually *like* talking about happens to also be the thing that people like to joke about. And if they don't joke about it, their eyes glaze over like I'm boring them to death.

"Needed a break to keep those creative juices flowing," I tell him.

"Sure, man," Mason says, his eyes quickly darting down

to the cooler I'm carrying. "Bruh! What'd you bring us? Any beers in there?"

"Andie's mom is here, dude, chill." Patrick smacks Mason in the pec, and Bekah laughs.

At the mention of her name, I scan the beach for Andie. The pin she dropped wasn't all that helpful in figuring out her exact location on the beach. We're gonna have to work on that. And when she proposed the Deal last night on the dock, she didn't get into any particulars on whether or not this arrangement was something we'd be keeping under wraps. We didn't talk about how we'd explain it to our friends when they inevitably start to wonder why the two of us are suddenly hanging out after spending years just passing each other by, either.

So, I'm not exactly sure how to explain the reason for me bringing a cooler of drinks and snacks for no one else but me and Andie. In a moment of panic, I settle for something I don't do often, and I lie.

"Nah, man. My laptop's in there," I say, attempting to keep a straight face. "It's a hack to keep it from overheating in the sun."

"Oh-kaaaay," Mason says as three pairs of eyes stare blankly at me like I've just sprouted a baby alien from my neck.

I take the awkward moment I've created as my opportunity to escape. After dropping my paddleboard by the tent, I head down to the shore. On my way, I shoot Andie a text.

Me: just got to the beach

Me: U still here?

Andie: Who dis?

Her reply makes me stop in my tracks. We saved our numbers in each other's phones before we left the dock last night. At this point I realize that even though I've known Andie for years, I don't *know her* know her. Not that well, at least. She could be joking right now, or she could have been joking last night. But before I can text her back, my phone vibrates in my hand.

Andie: Kidding! I know who u r Tommy Ling

Andie: But I don't see u

Me: just left Mason's tent

Me: I'll come to u. wru?

Andie: w my mom by the rock wall

Andie: She's about to head home

Me: omw over

ndie's hair is tied up on top of her head, with dark strands of tight curls falling around her face. And here I am wondering if it gets annoying to have all that hair blowing around in the breeze, tickling your nose and cheeks and shoulders.

"So, what's your ex-girlfriend's name?"

We've been sitting alone on two warm beach towels by the rock wall for less than five minutes. I was doing my thing, quietly observing, when she just sideswiped me with this question. It probably shows on my face too, because when Andie looks up at me, her cheeks flush bright pink, and she cringes.

"Wow! I'm sorry," she says between bites of the dried mango I brought for her. "Guess I suck at the whole distracting-you-from-your-heartbreak assignment, huh?"

I reach over and snag a slice of mango from the plastic bag she's holding. "Unless you're trying to do some experimental reverse-psychology thing where you try to get me to *stop* thinking about my ex by asking me biographical details *about* my ex, then I'd say there's room for improvement," I tell her before taking a bite of the tangy, leathery fruit.

She laughs. Not in a soft, cute way like she's flirting with me. But in a full-throated *I couldn't care less if my nostrils are flaring* way. And suddenly I'm smiling back at her. That's when I notice her eyes scan past my face and land somewhere behind me down the beach. I turn around to find Patrick and Bekah goofing off in the water.

It's like a scene from one of those cheesy reality-dating shows. Bekah's splashing him in the face, pretending like she's trying to get away. Patrick catches her and lifts her over his shoulder to spin her around. I won't lie. It is kind of sickening. They could be the stars of an ad for bubble gum, or life after a positive herpes diagnosis. Their over-the-top laughter floats on the breeze until it reaches us here in our private misery hole by the rocks.

When I turn back to Andie, I'm prepared to make a joke to smooth over the sting of having to witness the whole display. But she's not watching them anymore.

Instead she's closely examining the sand—tracing small circles with her index finger. Her brows are drawn tight, and her mouth is twisted to the side. It's obvious she's in her head.

Then it hits me like a dead fish. Andie only asked me about Chloe to get her mind off what's happening on this beach—the guy she wants, completely wrapped up in a girl who's not her. I'd bet the hundred bucks Mason still owes me that Patrick and Bekah's PDA has been the main attraction on the beach today and is the reason for Andie's SOS text. I'm not usually this slow on the uptake, but it is my first day on the gig as a wingman. So I give myself some grace. And now that I've put it all together, I can take my cue.

"Her name is Chloe," I tell Andie. "We met last year in AP English."

"Ooooh," Andie says. "So she's a nerd like you."

"Yeah," I sigh. "But she had her faults."

Andie's eyes light up, and she shifts on the blanket, revealing a peek of her orange bathing suit under her cover-up. "Spill! We love a tortured genius."

I avert my eyes and rub my chin, pretending to think about her question. "Well, for starters," I say, "Chloe ate her pizza crust first."

Andie gasps. "Who *does* that?"

"Oh, but it gets worse," I tell her.

She laughs. "How could it?"

"Whenever she sneezed, she'd scream."

Andie's eyebrows crinkle in the middle like she's confused. "Wait, what? Like a high-pitched squeak, or are we talking bloodcurdling yelp?"

"Not the squeak," I confirm. "One time we almost got put out of a movie theater because she was allergic to the cushions and couldn't stop sneeze-screaming for, like, ten minutes."

Andie's mouth drops into an O shape. Then we both burst into laughs. "Oh my God!" she says with a snort. "I'm sorry, but I'd pay to see that."

We laugh for a few more seconds, and then we fade into silence. I'm watching the water, thinking about how good it felt to have someone to go to the movies with—even if we caused a public disturbance while we were at it.

Andie is resting her chin on her knees now, still drawing those small circles in the sand. But a tiny smile starts to push up the corners of her mouth. "I'm sorry Chloe broke your heart, Tommy." Her words are soft and quiet, but I can tell she means them.

"It's all part of the game, I guess," I say, shrugging off the dull pain in my chest. "You know how people say 'Better to have love and lost than never to have loved at all,' or something like that?"

Andie turns her face to mine, one eyebrow raised. "You really believe that?" she asks dryly.

"I don't know." I take a swig of my Snapple and look

out over the water. "I do know that I don't regret being with Chloe, even if I'm not anymore. If that makes sense?"

"I wonder if my mom feels that way about my dad," Andie says. And then her eyes screw shut. She groans, covering her face with her hands. I can tell she wishes she could unsay it. "Ugh! Sorry. I shouldn't have taken it there. Too depressing."

"It's okay," I jump in, even though I have no idea how to have *this* conversation. I'm barely prepared to help her get over my brother, let alone *this*. I know what it's like to be part of a breakup, but I have no idea what it's like to watch your parents fall apart. I feel like whatever I say right now won't be enough. But I try anyway.

"I . . . I was sorry to hear about your parents," I tell her. And that plunges us into an awkward silence.

Patrick and I learned that Mr. and Mrs. Weaver had called it quits sometime between last summer and this one when my parents couldn't stop talking about it on the drive up the mountain earlier this week. I guess Andie's mom called our mom a few days before vacation to update her on their new "family dynamic," as Mom put it. Mom vowed to get all the details from Ms. Veronica at our family's Summer Kickoff party. But Andie's mom never showed up. And Dad said he'd give Mr. David a call to "check in" once we'd gotten settled for the summer.

Back home in Santa Barbara, over half of my friends' parents are broken up, and some are even on their second or third rounds of marriage. But from the outside looking in, I didn't ever expect Andie's parents to be on that list. Like puzzle pieces, I always felt like they just made sense together. Hearing about their split was almost as much of a shock to me as Chloe's breakup text. And the way Andie's face falls when she thinks about her parents is a clear sign that Patrick's not the only one who's broken her heart this summer.

"I have an idea," I say, screwing on the top to my Snapple and sliding it back into the cooler. Then, after hopping up to my feet, I reach for Andie's hand. "You trust me?"

The very skeptical look in her eyes says, *That depends.* Still, she slowly puts her Snapple and the mangoes back into the cooler and allows me to tug her up from the sand.

"Where exactly are we going?" she asks as we start to pack up our things.

"It's a surprise," I say. "But it will be fun. I promise."

The place I have in mind is one of my favorite spots on the mountain. I scan the beach, looking for her usual accomplice—something tells me that taking Andie there alone isn't the best idea. Someone might spot us and make assumptions. People are already talking about her parents' divorce. The last thing Andie needs is a lake scandal with rumors about a love triangle with brothers when that is *so* not what this is.

"Mel around?" I ask.

"She's up there with Augie," she answers, pointing toward the rock wall.

I look that way and find them cuddled together, watching something on Augie's phone. I whistle to get their attention. "Hey! You two want to get outta here?"

Mel glances up and gawks at me, which is fair, because I've started all of maybe two conversations with her in the years that we've been aware of each other's existence. One was last night in the bunk room, and the other probably went something like *Hey, can you pass the mustard?*

Mel looks to Andie like she's in the process of being kidnapped and asks, "Andie, is this man bothering you?"

Andie laughs and throws an arm over my shoulder. It's awkward because I've easily got her by six or seven inches. Her arm is tiny, but just like with her palm on my forearm last night, her skin is soft and warm. "No! Tommy's just . . . He's helping me out with some stuff this summer."

"That's not suspicious at all," Mel deadpans. But she starts making her way down the rocks, with Augie following close behind her. And just like that, we've got our crew for my little adventure.

TOMMY

The swimming hole at Azure Falls is my summertime happy place. In the winter, it's frozen over, which makes hiking there nearly impossible. But every summer since I turned fourteen and was old enough to find this place on a map, I've come here whenever I've needed to get away. Usually I'll hike here alone with my music and my notepad, or sometimes nothing at all. This summer, I planned to bring Chloe up to show her my bit of paradise.

Unfortunately, I'm not the only one knows about this magic spot on the mountain, because by the time we get there, about a dozen other people have beat us to it. Some of them are sunbathing, some are swimming, and a handful are currently making the climb up to the ledge by the waterfall—ready to take the thirty-foot plunge.

We reach the clearing, and a perfect view of the swimming hole and waterfall opens up in front of us. I've seen it dozens of times, and it never gets old. I look over at Andie, who's facing skyward and turning in a circle to take in all the trees—specks of sunlight dotting her face through the canopy. She's quiet, but I can tell she's impressed.

I startle when August claps me on the back and jostles my shoulder. "Dude, this is legit!" he says, before turning to his girlfriend. "Babe, how did we not know about this place?"

Mel jabs me in the rib. "Tommy's clearly been holding out on us."

I wince away from the sharp little weapons at the ends of her fingers. "Jeez, Mel. What are those, talons?"

"Close enough." She shrugs, admiring her nail art. "They're Gel-X. So don't cross me." She winks, clawing at me with them.

I'm about to ask what the hell "Gel-X" means when a long high-pitched shout followed by the unmistakable splash of a body hitting the water steals our attention from all talk of Mel's stabby nails.

"Uhhh," Andie chimes in for the first time since we got here. "You guys aren't actually going to climb up there and jump, are you?"

Oh shit. I'll admit I don't know *a lot* about Andie Weaver—that's been my brother's territory for the past four summers. After last night, it's confirmed that she's got a weak stomach. I didn't consider that she might also have a fear of heights. If I had, I certainly wouldn't have brought her here.

Augie shrugs, oblivious to Andie's discomfort. "I'll do it if Mel does," he says, looking over at his girlfriend.

Mel loops an arm through Andie's, and the two of them seem to have a silent conversation with their eyes. When Mel looks back at me and Augie, she says, "It's okay, guys. I'll hang back with my girl."

"No, no, no, no, no, no, no! I'm good. I can do it. I mean, *we* can do this. All of us can!" Andie insists.

She's got no one convinced. First off, the color has drained from her face and her pupils are as wide as hockey pucks. Next, she's taking these fast and shallow breaths—like she could hyperventilate any moment now.

I toss a worried look at Mel, who's looking back at me the same way. I should probably figure out a game plan fast, since I'm the one who brought us here promising "fun."

"Okay," I say, "how about we just swim first and work our way up to the jump? Nobody's in a rush, right?"

"Nope!" Mel says, looking at Augie. "We got nothin' but time. Come on, babe, let's get wet!" She grabs his hand, and they head off toward the swimming hole.

"Okay, good. This is good," Andie says, reassuring herself. And at the prospect of not having to dive this very second, the color floods back to her face, and instantly her breathing slows.

"You doing okay there, champ? Or do I need to grab a bucket?" I tease, trying to lighten the mood. She throws me a scowl and marches ahead to the water's edge.

I follow, and once we get there, we strip down to our suits and head in. Augie does a cannonball while Mel executes a perfect swimmer's dive into the crystal-blue pool. Unlike our showboat friends, Andie and I just wade in, letting our bodies slowly adjust to the cool temperature of the water. We're knee-deep when Andie breaks the silence.

"You come here often?" she asks through chattering teeth.

"Is that a pickup line?" I shoot back at her, hoping to dust off any leftover bits of her almost panic attack.

"No, you weirdo," she says, splashing me in the chest. I wince at the ice-cold sensation. "God forbid a girl try to get to know her wingman."

"Yes, I come here often," I admit. "That was kind of a clumsy save earlier, by the way. Telling Mel I'm helping you with 'some stuff' this summer. We should probably come up with a better cover if we aren't going to tell them the truth."

Andie seems to think about it for a beat. "You're a writer, right?" she asks, and it catches me by surprise. I've never talked to her about the book I've been trying to write since sophomore year of high school. Obviously, she heard about it from Patrick. I wonder what kinds of jokes he's made about it with her.

I realize several seconds have passed in silence and I still haven't answered her. Clearing my throat, I say, "Um, yeah. I mean, I like to write," sounding not at all confident. "What does that have to do with us?"

"Well, you're a writer, and I assume you're good at it from all the time you spend with your computer," she says. "I'm applying early decision to Stanford and need to perfect my essay. So we *could* tell our friends that you're helping me out with it. That's believable, right?"

"Yeah. That's good," I say, because I can't really think up anything better.

Another person shouting as they free-fall off the ledge cuts into our conversation, redirecting our attention. "I've lost count of the number of times I've made that leap," I say.

She doesn't reply. So I turn and watch her look up at the sparkling waterfall. I notice the lean muscles in her neck moving along with the giant gulp she takes.

"You don't like heights?" I ask, even though it's practically obvious at this point. By now, we're waist-deep and I'm famil-iar enough with this swimming hole that I know in a couple of feet there's a drop-off where we'll have to tread water.

"I prefer to say that heights don't like *me*," she corrects, stretching her arms up and basking in the sunlight that peeks through the opening at the center of the thick canopy of trees. "I *want* to make peace with roller coasters, rooftops . . . hell, even the winding drive up this gigantic mountain every summer and winter. But anytime I try, I get this queasy feeling in my stomach. I mean . . ." She gives me a look. "There has been puke."

"You don't say," I mumble.

"Hey, now!" She cuts her eyes at me with a smirk.

That's when I get the idea. Andie sent me the SOS because she needed a distraction from Patrick and Bekah's PDA show on the beach. And what better distraction than conquering one of your biggest fears?

"Well, maybe this can be another thing I can wingman for you this summer." I point to the ledge by the waterfall. "How do we get you up there without . . . you know." I assume she can finish the sentence.

She's quiet, just staring at the waterfall while another climber takes their jump. Suddenly her face lights up and she gasps. "I know!" she says, pulling off the bandanna that she's been wearing as a headband. "Here." She turns her back to me before suggesting, "You can lead me up there blindfolded and push me off!"

Laughing, I put my hands on her shoulders and spin her back around to face me. "Slow your roll," I say. "I don't want to go to jail for kidnapping, Andie."

Smiling, she reaches up to pat me on the cheek. "Well, that was just my first idea, Tommy. We're only spitballing here."

All I can do is smile, because at least she doesn't seem as terrified as she did five minutes ago.

"Here's the plan," I tell the group. "We're all going to start the climb together. I'll take lead. Girls, you'll go in the middle. Augie, you bring up the rear." I lock eyes with him, and he nods. "When we get up to the ledge, Augie, you and Mel can jump together. And, Andie, you're with me. How does that sound?"

"Beautiful, Tommy," Mel says before leaning up to kiss Augie on the cheek.

"Aye-aye, Captain," he says, saluting me. For a second, I wonder what Chloe would think of me in this moment. Is this the Tommy she wanted?

Then I look at Andie. The pale, bug-eyed look has returned to her face. All the confidence I had in my plan a second ago starts to drain out of me.

"You don't have to do it, Andie," Mel tells her. "You can hang back and we'll meet you back down here."

The second she makes that suggestion, I can see the spark of fire in Andie's eyes. She's afraid, sure. But she's also determined to do this. And I'm determined to help her not be a bystander, just like I promised.

"I've got her, Mel," I say, placing a hand on Mel's shoulder. I look at Andie. "If we get up there and you don't want to jump, I'll climb back down with you."

She nods and smiles, and we all make our way to the base of the rock wall to start our climb.

It takes us about ten minutes to get to the top. The ledge is high, but the climb is gradual and manageable enough without shoes. About halfway up, after the second time Andie asks for a break, it seems like a good idea for Mel and Augie to go on ahead. We let them pass, and for the rest of the way I don't take my eyes off Andie, who's climbing ahead of me now.

"Just a few more steps and we're there," I call up to her.

"You said that an hour ago!" she shouts, turning back. When she gets a glimpse of the drop-off, she immediately starts to wilt.

I catch her and slowly bring her down to sit on the rocks. "First of all, we haven't even been here that long," I say with a laugh, hoping to lighten the mood.

She glances at my wrist. "You don't have a watch, Tommy. How would *you* know?"

I lift her chin so she's looking me in the eye when I say this: "Andie, we really don't have to do this," I tell her.

"Wrong," she says forcefully. "I'm doing this, Tommy. We said we wouldn't spend the summer letting life just happen to us. Jumping off this slab of earth is me taking life by the horns and—"

Instead of finishing that sentence, Andie lurches forward with a dry heave.

I rub her back as she stares at the ground and collects herself. Andie seems so tough and unflappable in some ways—I've seen her absolutely wipe the floor with my brother during beach soccer. This is a completely different side of her. I resist the urge to brush the curls away from her face. We're friends now, but not friends like *that*.

Andie finally sits up straight, presses a hand to her stomach, and pinches the bridge of her nose. "It's okay. I'm okay. That was a false alarm."

I'm staring at her like she's a chick hatching from an egg. I don't know if I've seen a person so determined despite the odds. Still, I can't in good conscience watch this happen. What was I thinking? I stand and gently pull her up with me.

"Look, we'll head back down and just try this another day," I say. "We almost made it to the ledge. That's not nothing."

Without a word, she snatches her hand from my grasp and brushes past me. I stay where I am, watching her. She marches up to the drop-off.

Turning around to pierce me with a determined look, she says, "Tommy, I'm doing this. Are you with me?"

I release a heavy sigh, because she's clearly a free agent. I step up next to her. I look her in the eye. "On the count of three, we jump together. Okay?"

She nods enthusiastically. All the paleness and queasiness and near puking from seconds ago has disappeared. I'm impressed, and a little bit terrified—*for her.*

I take a deep breath and start the count. We're side by side.

"One." Andie is looking at me. I give her a nod. We've got this.

"Two." Her gaze is down at the water, her knees bending a bit in anticipation.

"Three." I turn my attention to the water, and I jump.

For five seconds, I'm weightless in the air. Splashes of water from the nearby falls spray me as I fall feetfirst. I make contact and plunge deep into the pool. I open my eyes underwater hoping for a glimpse of Andie. But there's no one. When I break through the surface, I whip my head to the left and right, and still there's no sign of her.

Panicked, I call her name. Once. Then twice, before she calls back.

"Up here!"

The sound comes from high above me. Wiping my wet hair from my eyes, I glance up and see a sliver of her bright orange bikini peeking out from behind the ledge.

She panicked. She didn't jump.

CHAPTER FOURTEEN

"Well, if it isn't Mel-Bell and Andie-Bug gracing us with their presence!" Sylvia, the aging but ever-fabulous owner and manager of the Village Sweet Shoppe greets us as we enter. "You girls breaking hearts this summer or what?"

Smiling and arm in arm, we make our way to the case of delectable ice cream flavors. "Ms. Sylvia, you know I'm taken these days," Mel reminds her. "I only have eyes for Augie Masterson."

"Ah! That boy's a sweetheart," Ms. Sylvia practically coos. "He and his daddy been coming around to fix up this place, and I just know they're not charging me the going rates."

"That's my Augie," Mel says proudly.

"And what about you, little Miss Weaver?" Ms. Sylvia asks. "You and that Ling boy finally stop playing around and make it official?"

"Oh, Patrick? He's just a friend. Not my type *at all*," I insist, adding the lie and waving my hand like I never thought we could be anything more. Like I haven't, as recently as this very week, lost sleep over the fact that I fumbled my chance and now he's moved on to better, taller, raspier-voiced things.

"Well, then, what about the other one?" Ms. Sylvia says, completely throwing me off. "I always thought the older one . . . What's his name?" she asks, and I don't dare offer the answer. "Tommy!" she remembers. "Yes, Tommy Ling. He's a real catch, if you ask me. It's the quiet ones that will often surprise you. Take my Leonard, for example. We'll be married fifty years in October."

Mel nudges me hard in the side, and I rush to order my rocky road.

"Okay, time to spill! You know that Ms. Sylvia's basically a clairvoyant. Plus, what the heck was yesterday all about?"

Mel pins me in place with hard-set eyes. While our moms finish up another marathon thrifting run, we're sitting on the rainbow-colored hand-shaped chairs out in front of Ms. Sylvia's shop, eating ice cream. I have a feeling Mel's mom is grilling mine on all things *divorce* in the same way her daughter's going to interrogate me about my special arrangement with Tommy Ling.

Mel's not going to fall for the "college essay" excuse. So, I surrender to my fate and figure it's safe enough to let her in on what's really going on. With a heavy sigh, I spill the beans. "You know the night of the Lings' party, how you couldn't find me for a while after beer pong?"

"Oh my God!" Mel shouts, leaning forward, her jaw hanging open. "You snuck off to hook up with Patrick's brother?"

"Shh!" I clap my free hand over her mouth and glance around, making sure no one heard. She bats my hand away and grins.

Mel's suggestion plants a vivid image in my mind of Tommy Ling standing too close to me on the dock and leaning down too far. I see his dark hair. It's wavier and slightly longer than Patrick's. Then his eyes. Green instead of brown. His dimples sink deeper into both cheeks. And then his lips. Fuller. Broader. I never really thought much of it, but Tommy's *everything* is just a bit more intense than his brother's. I shake my head to blur the image and get the thought of him hovering close enough to kiss me out of my mind. Because, what the hell is that even about?

"Of course not," I say, reaching up to wipe the random sweat on my temple. "Who do you think I am? And what do you think this is, *The Vampire Diaries*?"

Mel relaxes back into her chair that's shaped like a hand, taking a long lick off her chocolate cone. "Well, you can't blame me for jumping to conclusions," she says quite casually. "That night was a shit show. And I love you, but you *were* kind of doing the most."

Ignoring the fact that for the majority of the night, Mel was right there "doing the most" beside me, I get back to explaining. "Tommy and I did *not* hook up. We just *talked.* On the dock. For, like, . . . an hour."

Her eyes go wide. "Andie." She gasps. "That's a big deal."

"What's so special about that?"

Mel adjusts in her seat to face me directly. "As far as we know, Tommy is a late teen of the cis-het-male variety," she explains. "Before Augie, do you know what I've had to subject myself to in order to get even a fifteen-minute conversation out of one of *them*?" she asks with genuine shock and awe. Mel then leans forward, propping her elbow on the thumb of the chair and resting her chin on her fist. "What did you even talk about? Teach me your ways."

"Well, first, he just apologized again for ruining my kiss on the beach with Patrick last summer."

Mel grimaces. "That was embarrassing."

"Yes. I know," I say. "Then he started telling me about his recent breakup. And it hit me that we're both kind of the oddballs out this summer."

At this point, Mel's eyes catch a spark, and she sits up

straight. "Oh my God! You're doing it! Tell me you're fake dating him. This is my absolute favorite trope. You know this."

I'm about to say I thought it was enemies to lovers, but instead I raise my hands to pump her brakes. "No! *No*," I say. "It's way less complicated than that. Me and Tommy are just . . . I don't know, being there for each other. We're like . . ." I pause, searching for the right words, and all I can come up with is "Serving as each other's heartbreak-support animals for the summer."

Mel raises her eyebrows slowly, like I've just given her the elevator pitch for a cult I recently joined. Then her mouth drops into a frown.

"But . . . I thought *I* was your heartbreak-support animal. I thought I was your *general* support animal."

It didn't cross my mind that Mel's feelings could get hurt by the fact that I've chosen to lean on Tommy for help moving on from Patrick this summer. But now that it's obvious that it has, on instinct, I reach out for her hand. "And you are!" I say, reassuring her. "It's just . . ." I pause, because this part is going to be hard for me to say. "Well . . . you have Augie. And it took a lot for you two to get here," I explain.

"You're right," she admits. "That kid has crushed hard on me since I was taller than him."

"And you barely gave him an ounce of attention," I remind her.

She sighs, a huge smile stretching across her face. "To

think, all it took was a blizzard and an avalanche for me to see the light."

It's hard for me to not smile back. "Now you can't get enough of the guy."

Last year over the winter holiday, both of their families got snowed in for a whole week past Christmas on the mountain. This left enough time for Mel to cozy up to the idea that maybe she had more feelings for August than she'd realized.

"This is your first summer together, and you two deserve to have the best time," I tell her. "Without me moping around like some lumpy third wheel."

"But, Andie, you know it's hoes before bros over here," Mel insists. "I mean, don't get me wrong. Augie is bae. But you and me, we *always* come first. You know that, right?"

"I do know that. And believe me, I'm not ditching you for Tommy," I say. "He's just somebody who can understand what I'm going through right now. And I guess I'm that somebody for him too. And also, after a couple of conversations . . . I realize that he's kind of like an onion. He's got layers to peel back."

Mel smirks like she's just opened a steaming pot of hot tea. But she keeps her mouth shut, returning to her quickly melting ice cream cone.

"What?" I ask.

"Oh, nothing," she muses. "First it's 'He's an onion,' and then it's 'Mel, I'm not a virgin anymore!'"

She says the last part so loudly and with so much flare

that a lady walking into the Sweet Shoppe stares at us, her brows drawn close and her mouth open with alarm. I give the lady a polite, innocent smile and wave before aiming wide eyes at my friend. "Gah, Mel! You're going to have all of Big Bear discussing my very *nonexistent* sex life," I say, laughing.

"Oh, please," she says, totally unbothered. "That was Mrs. Cornblatt. Chances are she's going home with her pint of vanilla bean to a smutty book after that."

Laughing, I roll my eyes and dive back into my rocky road with rainbow sprinkles.

"You've got to be kidding me," Mom says as we pull up to our lake house after finishing our afternoon shopping in town.

"Roni, tell me that's not Simon Rodriguez on your front porch, now, is it?" Mel's mom asks from the front passenger seat. She's leaning so far forward, her forehead almost reaches the windshield.

When I look up at the house, sure enough, there's the man in question standing on the top step of the porch. A second ago he had his arms crossed with one shoulder pressed against one of our wooden columns, but when he notices Mom's Subaru pulling up toward the driveway, he straightens, pushing his hands into the pockets of his weathered jeans.

From my spot in the back seat, I can hear the deep breath and exhale that my mom takes. Mel reaches across the middle seat to squeeze my knee. We lock eyes, and there's no doubt that we're both thinking about the conversation we attempted to have with my mom in our kitchen—the one where she totally avoided spilling the beans on her one-sided beef with Simon Rodriguez.

I honestly haven't been able to stop thinking about it. So many questions have popped up for me since. I've wanted to ask my mom, but she's basically a steel trap. The universe must be on my side now, because the guy's on our front porch.

By the time Mom throws the car into park, my head is swimming with potential reasons for why he showed up here today. Maybe he's living under a rock, doesn't know my parents are divorced, and came to smoke a cigar with my dad—unlikely. Maybe he knows my dad isn't here and finally sees a shot with Mom and wants to take it—intriguing.

When we exit the car, Mel and her mom take their bags and head across the street to their house while me and Mom turn toward our porch. Simon calls out to us as he walks down the steps to meet us halfway. "Hey, ladies, sorry to surprise you," he says, his voice deep. "Can I help you with your bags?"

Mom offers him a tight smile and a nervous laugh. And I do a double take because I'm not used to seeing her like this—jittery and unsure of herself. Either she hates him or she likes him. Gotta be one of the two. And I'm for whichever outcome stops Mom from adding to her questionably large collection of antique bear figurines.

"Um. Yes . . ." She stumbles over her words as her eyes dart between the two of us. "Thanks, Simon."

The three of us walk together in silence, and I'm wondering if he's going to tell us what he's doing here. I'm about to ask when Mom's the first to break the ice.

"So, what brings you over to our side of the lake today?" she asks. "David's not coming up till at least the fall."

I'm walking a step or two behind them, and at the mention of my dad's name, Simon's shoulders tense. Mental note taken.

"Oh, I know. I was actually hoping I'd get a chance to talk with you, Veronica." He reaches up to scratch his beard, eyes never leaving Mom's face. "Promise it won't take long."

The intimate way her first name floats off his lips makes me feel like I should be seeing myself out of this conversation. But we're on the porch at the front door, with them on either side of it and me front and center. It's awkward, to say the least. I wish I could blink and just disappear into the wooden planks. That way I could listen without them knowing and take all my notes back to Mel. At the same time, I don't know how many secrets I can keep before I explode. I still haven't told Mom about the ring Dad bought for Trishell. She could take it as a wake-up call to go out and start a new version of her life. Or she could spiral and go out and get more bears.

Mom looks at me with a face I can't quite read. I'm not sure if she wants to be rescued from Simon or set free. "Honey, do you mind taking all of this inside while we talk out here on the porch?" she asks.

"No problem," I say, offering her a smile. I can tell she's nervous, and I wish I could hug her without it seeming over-the-top. I settle for a wink instead.

"It's good seeing you, Andie," Simon says with a smile just as I'm unlocking the door.

I turn back and offer him a small smile in return. "You too, Mr. Simon."

When I'm inside, I drop the bags, lean my back against the front door, and let the air whoosh out of me. The last five minutes have felt like a full day of binge-watching a mur-der mystery, and my nerves are completely shot. Now I'm wondering if that old trick of holding a cup up to the door so I can eavesdrop really works. Then my pocket vibrates. I assume it's an anxious text from Mel, who's probably spying on Mom and Simon from her living room window. But it's not her.

Fool me once, shame on you. Fool me twice, shame on me. But what are the rules for random drive-by texting from your ex?

My baseball cap arrived in the mail this morning in a crumpled-up package without even a note, so getting another text from Chloe was definitely not on my summer bingo card.

For weeks I've had dreams of her showing up on the front doorstep of the lake house with a suitcase, ready to confess it was all a mistake. Saying she wanted me back and we could spend the summer together like we'd planned. I've had other dreams too. Ones about going back to Santa Barbara and running into her around the Funk Zone. Only, those were more like nightmares. Because in them, she wasn't alone. She was with some new guy with ear gauges and neck tats and all their new friends who are "easy to be around."

I foolishly kept a sliver of hope alive that I'd hear from her again. But I didn't *really* expect it.

Chloe: Saw this today and thought of the look on your face that time we got locked out of your car at the baseball field 💀

Chloe: btw did you get the hat?

I miss you. I'm sorry. Those are the five words I've been waiting, hoping to see reflecting back at me in electric-blue light. Not some awkward small talk about old memories. But maybe hearing *something* from her is better than nothing?

Within seconds, my fingers are moving across the screen.

Me: SOS

When Andie's footsteps start to echo down the dock, I quickly save my Word document and close out of the app. I'm still working on Sonam and Maxis's sentencing scene in the king's court. But ever since Chloe's text came through, figuring it all out has felt like looking for a quarter at the bottom of a sandbox in one-hundred-degree weather.

Andie plops down next to me and lets her legs dangle down toward the water. Today she's wearing denim shorts and a flowy white shirt. Her hair hangs free, blowing in the breeze off the lake. I've always known that Andie was pretty, in the same way I know that tacos are a superior food option. But in the past week I've started to really zero in on the "why"—like the details in a story that make a character feel alive on a page.

Because now I'm noticing things like the way Andie's eyes aren't just hazel. They're fireworks of color with these tiny specks of gold that make them shine in the light. And even when her smile stretches wide across her face, her lips are still full and cinnamon-colored and—

"A penny for your thoughts?" she says, and the question interrupts my study of the freckles that spread across her nose. I wonder if she noticed me trying to count them.

I clear my throat. "Sorry, what was that?" I ask, rubbing the beads of sweat that just broke out on the back of my neck.

"I *said*, a penny for your thoughts?" she repeats. She reaches over and presses a real penny into my palm. I clasp it, accidentally catching her fingers.

"Thanks," I say, meeting her eyes.

"For good luck," she says, gently pulling her hand back.

I sigh and look out at the water. "Think I'm gonna need it."

"You okay, Tommy?" She reaches up to place her palm on my forehead. "The heat getting to you or something?"

I laugh and swat at her hand, ducking out of the way. "I'm fine," I insist. "I just, uh . . . well, I got this." I figure since we've promised to be in this together, I might as well show her the text. I dig into my pocket to hand Andie my phone so she can see Chloe's message. When she reads it, she claps a hand over her mouth.

"This is . . ." Andie gasps. "I mean, this is good, right? Isn't it, like, the dream to have the person who stomped on your heart come crawling back begging for forgiveness?"

I look at her, rubbing the back of my neck again. "I guess?" I shrug. "Also, let's not get carried away. She didn't say all that."

"Finding a random excuse to text you is classic regretful-ex behavior. Trust me," Andie says. "It's confusing, I know. First, she dumps you. Now she, what? Wants you back? It's whiplash. I get why you're spiraling."

"I wouldn't call it spiraling . . ."

"Well, you did send the SOS. Which means you needed to be rescued," she argues. "You can be honest with me, Tommy. Even I can admit that I was spiraling watching Patrick and Bekah make out on the rocks, and in the sand, and in the water, and—"

"Okay, okay. I get the picture," I say, trying to scrub from my mind the images of my brother and his girlfriend sucking face. As if I haven't seen enough of that already.

"What are you gonna say back?" Andie asks, shoving the phone back into my hands. Is she imagining what it would be like to get this kind of text from Patrick?

"I have no idea," I admit. "What would *you* say?"

Andie mulls for a beat. "Well . . . I think it all depends," she says after several seconds. "You could text back something like *I got the hat. Thanks. When can we talk?* Or . . ."

"Or?"

She bites her lip, thinking again. "Or . . . since our pact *is* about moving on, if you haven't changed your mind, you could say, *new phone, who dis*?"

I laugh. But neither option feels quite right. "You got anything else?" I ask.

Andie twists her lips and loops a long dark coil of hair around her finger. Her nails are short and round—not stabby like Mel's. They're bright purple too. And the paint is slightly chipped.

When I realize I am, once again, staring at the details, I look away.

"You don't have to decide right now," she finally answers. "You can leave Chloe on read until you figure out exactly what you want to say."

The second Andie suggests it, the tight squeeze in my chest starts to release its hold. Ever since Chloe's come back from ghost land, finding the right way to respond to her has felt like some massive, urgent task. But the truth is, it's not. She dumped me and went no-contact. Now she's back. I can take my time with this.

"Thanks, Andie," I tell her. It's simple, but I mean it.

She smiles. And it's that wide, bright, and full smile. Then she shrugs. "That's what heartbreak-support animals are for."

I feel my brows come together. "Um. What was that?" I ask.

"A heartbreak-support animal . . . I've decided that's what we are to each other," she explains, eyes wide, gesturing between the two of us. "I made it up when I was explaining our arrangement to Mel. I kind of prefer that to being called your wing-woman." She looks adorably pleased with herself.

I laugh. "You're different, Andie Weaver" is all I manage to say back to her.

"I'll take that as a compliment," she says, smiling.

"You should." Then I absorb what she's just said. "Wait . . . so Mel knows about our deal?"

"I'm sorry for blowing up our spot," she says, briefly putting her hand on my knee. "But after you took us on that hike to jump to our deaths, Mel got curious. She thought we'd been hooking up!" Andie says, and the way she emphasizes the words *hooking up* makes the idea sound utterly ridiculous. "So, I had to fill her in. You know, so she doesn't get the wrong idea. I mean, can you *imagine*?"

Can I imagine? I'm writing a novel set in a completely fantastical world. I can imagine *a lot* of things. But the exact scenario of me and Andie hooking up might turn out to be stranger than fiction. She's still into Patrick. Patrick used to be into her, at least enough to kiss her on a beach in front of all our friends. And me, well, I'm just the slightly older brother of the friend next door. And apparently the "heartbreak-support animal."

I'm also the guy who's been heartsick over his ex, who freezes whenever that ex texts him.

We're a mess.

"So . . . this book of yours," Andie says, and I wonder if she can read my mind. "You ever let anybody read it?"

I run my hands through my hair. No one has ever asked to see my writing before. Not even Chloe. The idea of people *actually* reading my stories is simultaneously one of my biggest dreams and greatest fears.

"No one's asked," I tell her honestly.

"Not even Chloe?" she asks, and the surprise in her voice scratches at a soft wound I didn't realize I had.

Suddenly I'm feeling defensive of my ex. "Dystopian romance isn't exactly her thing."

Andie's eyes go wide. "Wait . . . you're writing a romance?"

"A dystopian romance, yeah," I say. "Forbidden lovers get banished to an alternate timeline for defying the laws of the ruling class. But there's, like, action and stuff." I add that last part just in case Andie is going to judge me.

"So, you're saying there's time travel *and* sex?" she asks, her face splitting into a giant grin.

Nodding, I say, "There will be. Haven't gotten to the sex parts yet, though." What I don't say is the reason *why* I can't seem to get to those parts. That it's because whenever I start thinking about Sonam and Maxis having those moments of closeness, I can't help but think about the first time Chloe and

I had sex. And the times after that. She wasn't my first. But she's the only girl I've been with in a way that felt deeper than bodies and hormones. And I thought we'd have a lot more time to explore that part of our relationship. But I was wrong.

I could keep wallowing, but at this point, Andie is up on her knees, visibly excited. I'm worried she might fall into the lake. "Can I read them when you do? Hold on, no. I want to read the whole thing. Finished or not. Can I?"

Now it's my turn to be shocked. "Wait, what?"

"Me and Mel read each other's fic all the time," she says. And it comes off so casual, like she hasn't just blown my mind.

"You write fic?" I ask, surprising myself by my increased volume. "Patrick never said anything about that. Does he know?"

Andie shakes her head, and then her eyes drop. She realized she's just told me a secret. "Me and Mel started it a couple of years ago under a shared pen name."

I bury the sense of satisfaction at knowing something about Andie Weaver that even Patrick doesn't know. Then I switch topics because I have a question I've wanted to ask Andie for a couple of days now. "Have you tried . . . I don't know, *talking* to Patrick about what happened between you two last summer? I mean, apart from the sext you sent?"

"*It wasn't-a-sext!*" she squeaks out. She pins me with a serious stare to let me know she means business. "Don't ever bring the not-sext up again." Then she releases a heavy sigh. "And no, not yet," she admits. "Patrick and Bekah are always together. And I don't even know if it makes sense for me to try to talk to him about it now that he's with someone. Mama didn't raise a home-wrecker."

"Yeah," I say. "But you two were *really* good friends for so long. Seems like it would be kind of sad to just let that fade away without even a conversation. Don't you think?" Some closure with my brother might also help bring back some of that sparkle I'm used to seeing from her.

Andie seems to think about what I've just said as we sit in silence, watching the lake and the clouds and the boats and trees move at their own pace. The dock, like Azure Falls, is another one of my happy places on the mountain. Usually what makes my happy places so, well . . . happy is the fact that I can enjoy them by myself. But right now, being here with Andie, feels kind of nice. Like what it feels like to be easy to be around.

Because of that, I decide it's worth it to tell Andie the truth. "I think you should try to talk to him."

She looks confused, so I explain.

"We said we weren't just going to sit back and let the summer happen to us and that we were going to try to move on. So I think I know what our next challenge should be. I'll figure out what I'm going to say to Chloe and text her back. And you'll have a conversation with Patrick. Deal?"

Andie's mouth twists to the side, and I can tell she really doesn't want to agree to this.

"It'll be like jumping off the ledge. You were determined, remember?"

"Yeah, but I chickened out at the last second," she says, as if I needed reminding.

"Facts," I tell her, laughing. "So this time, don't." I shrug.

I see the moment she internally accepts the challenge, when she defiantly juts out her chin and nods just slightly. Andie then extends her hand to me, that familiar spark returning to her eyes. "You have a deal, Tommy Ling," she says. "Now back to you letting me read your sex scenes."

"Mom! Can you help me lace up the back of my dress?"

When she doesn't respond to my cry for help, I head down the hall between our two bedrooms. I can hear water running from her attached bathroom. She's still in the shower. Figuring I'll just catch her when she's out, I head into her room to raid her dresser for perfume and jewelry.

Tonight is the big swanky Independence Day party that Mel's parents host at their house every year. It's always a different vibe than the laid-back Juneteenth cookouts Mom hosts in our backyard in Santa Monica—but fun all the same.

The dress code asked for guests to come decked out in

red, white, or blue semiformal beach attire, and Mom's thrifting trip from last week came in clutch. For me, she found the perfect royal-blue maxi dress with a shimmery flowing skirt and straps that lace up the back. For herself, she scored a cherry-red dress with ruffled sleeves and a flirty skirt that skims her knees. We'll both be in matching strappy wedge heels to finish off our looks.

Usually I don't spend a lot of time on my hair and makeup. Chances are, I'm going to frizz it up or sweat it off, and plus, I'd rather wow the masses with my natural beauty anyway. But Tommy and I decided that tonight's the night I'm going to have the Talk with Patrick and he's going to text Chloe back. So these are special circumstances. Because what better night than the Fourth of July to free ourselves from the shackles of past and present regrets? We figured if things go south, at least there will be ample distraction around us in addition to the food and booze, so we can sneak away to eat and drink our feelings.

Even though I'm sold on the decision to talk it out with Patrick, every time I think about what I actually want out of this, things get a little fuzzy. Interfering with his and Bekah's relationship was never a real goal of mine. But I *do* want him to know that I'm sorry for ghosting him after we kissed. And that I want us to be friends again, like we were before. So, I'll take the confidence boost that mascara, highlighter, and setting spray provide. Plus, Mom's already singing along to

Beyoncé in the shower—and knowing she's having fun with getting glammed up for tonight feels really good.

Once I'm in her room, I go straight for her top dresser drawer because that's where she keeps the good stuff. When I open it, I'm surprised to find a folded piece of paper—the kind of paper you'd usually find in a notebook—on top of her jewelry tray. Traces of dark blue ink can be seen bleeding through the thin white page.

It's a letter.

Instant chills race down my arms, and I shoot a glance over my shoulder toward the bathroom to see if Mom's still showering. Not only is she still in there, but she's just made her way to favorites from the *Renaissance* album, which means I've got plenty of time.

If I wanted to, I could give the letter a quick skim and slip it back into place, and no one but me would know how sketchy I really am. Or I could grab a necklace, shut the drawer, and let the curiosity burn a whole in my brain for the rest of the night.

I consider these options for all of maybe three seconds before I snatch the letter and open it up. After a few words, my heart starts to race.

V—I'm sorry about everything. Since you won't return my calls, I figured writing to you was better than nothing . . .

"Andie, what are you doing?"

I jump and slam the drawer on my fingers. A flash of pain shoots through my hand, and I'm very close to blacking out—probably from shock *and* pain. She skipped the *Cowboy Carter* section of the playlist?

"Owwww!" I yelp. The letter falls to the ground, and I collapse with it.

"Sweetie, are you okay?" Mom rushes over to me while still wrapped in her towel. She reaches me and grabs for my hand, which is, unfortunately, bleeding. I clutch it to my chest.

"Honey, let me see," she says, gently pulling my hand over so she can inspect the damage. It looks like slamming my fingers in the drawer put a crack right in the center of the nail on my right middle finger.

"I'll get the first aid kit," Mom says, hurrying back into the bathroom.

All I can do is sit in my shame while resting my head in my hands—embarrassed, confused, finger throbbing. When Mom gets back, she gently cleans my finger and wraps it in a bandage. We don't say anything as she does the job. The whole time, the letter sits on the floor between us—the loudest object in the room.

When she's done, Mom closes up the first aid kit, adjusts the towel so it's tighter around her chest, and rests her hands on her bare knees.

"So," she says, "we should talk about what you saw."

"What if instead I just say sorry and we pretend it never happened?" I suggest. "I was just looking for your long gold chain, I swear. But then there it was. I figured it could be from Dad or . . ."

I trail off, not even knowing how to finish that sentence. By the look on Mom's face, I think she knows where it was going. She takes in a long deep breath and lets it out slowly. "Andie, did you read the letter?"

I shake my head. "I only got to the first line or two."

I can see the relief wash over my mom as all the tension drains from her face and her shoulders and arms relax. Suddenly the wild curiosity that had me tearing open the letter morphs into something a lot like regret. It may have something to do with the pain from my cracked fingernail, or realizing that maybe I'm not ready to be, like my grandma would say, "all up in grown folks' business."

But there is one thing I feel like I *have* to know.

"Mom, is the letter from Dad?" I ask. I had been too keyed up to analyze the handwriting, but it could have been his small, tight Dad scrawl.

"No, honey. It's not," she says. And when I suck in a sharp breath, I wonder if she knows how far I'm jumping to conclusions, because next she cups a hand to my face. "Andie, your dad and I never cheated on each other. That's not why we aren't together. I can't really explain everything for it to make sense. But I need you to understand that."

I nod. I know she wouldn't lie to me. Especially not about this. But if the letter wasn't from Dad, then who is it from?

"Your dad and I both had lives before we got together, and . . ." She pauses. "Marriage is hard. Love is hard. Life is hard. I think what I'm trying to say is, we're all just trying to figure things out as we go."

"I get it, Mom," I tell her. Even though it's only half-true. "I mean, at least I get the part about love being hard."

I might have said that with too much oomph, because now I feel the focus shift from her to me. "Sweetie, what's going on with you this summer?" Mom asks. "The situation with Patrick and Bekah still getting to you?"

I blow out a long breath. "I decided I'm going to talk to him tonight," I tell her, while fiddling with the shiny fabric of my skirt.

"Ah," Mom says, eyebrows rising. "I think that's great, sweetie. Know what you're going to say?"

"That—" I start, then stop to put my thoughts together. "That we never even got our chance to see if we could be more, you know? And it's mostly *my* fault. But now things are awkward since he's with her. And I don't know how or even if we can go back to before—"

"Honey." Mom stops me with a hand on my shoulder. "You don't have to be perfect or know all the right things to say," she explains. "You two have been friends for years. It's only a conversation. Just lead with how you feel."

When she puts it that way, I feel so much lighter. We talk for a bit more before I leave her room with the necklace I came for, a fresh wound, and a burning curiosity about the contents of that letter in her drawer.

Mom and I arrive at the party wrapped in our thrifted but chic tributes to American independence. Tawny Bridges scoops her up within seconds of us walking in their enormous oak door. After a quick hug and cheek kiss for me, Mrs. Bridges begins bombarding her with details about some tall tech guy in the kitchen that my mom absolutely *has to* meet.

As my mom gets carted away, she twists around to face me—her eyes shooting me a look that's part-amused, part-alarmed. "I'll find you later, honey," she promises before mouthing *You look gorgeous* at me over her shoulder. Between this and Mom's earlier pep talk, I'm feeling as ready as I'll ever be to finally tackle the elephant in the room called Patty.

The party's already packed, and so far no one has shunned the dress code. The house looks like someone tied a loose bag of patriotic Skittles to the ceiling fan and pressed the On switch. Mel already told me that when I got here she'd be outside on the dance floor with Augie. She also clued me in to the fact that Patrick and Bekah were there too.

It seems I have a habit of being fashionably late, which I don't mind. I always feel better slipping into a party that's already in full swing anyway. Less pressure to get the vibes going that way.

For now, I'm alone in the foyer, and there's one person whose location I have yet to confirm. And tonight, we're both on a mission with no room for error. I reach into my clutch for my phone, open up my messages with Tommy, and skim over our last exchange from about an hour ago.

Tommy: tonight's the night, grasshopper

Me: what did you just call me?

Tommy: I'm sorry

Tommy: tonight's the night . . . my queen

Me: much better. I'll allow it.

Smiling big, I type out another text to him.

Me: u here yet?

His response comes up in seconds.

Tommy: out back. U?

Me: just walked in. All systems go!

Tommy: we got this

After snaking my way through the crowded living and dining rooms, I pry open the glass doors that lead out to the back deck. Once outside, I get an elevated view of a dance floor on the lawn that's peppered with small groups and couples enjoying the music from a nearby DJ booth. I spot Mel and Augie at the edge of the black-and-white-checkered rectangle. She's got her phone camera set to record while he attempts the running man.

Mason and Evan are hanging around the DJ with Selina and Olivia. Patrick's at the bar with his hand resting on the small of Bekah's back. She's in a floor-length backless white maxi dress that looks both beachy *and* bridal.

As expected, everybody's paired up.

Suddenly my skin feels tight. I take a deep breath, shake off the jitters, and launch into the internal pep talk of a lifetime.

Andie, you're a badass bitch, and this summer you're up to hot-girl shit and hot-girl shit only! Who cares if she's in a wedding dress? Walk up to them. Smile. Say hi to her first. Then ask Patty if he can talk. Keep it cute and casual! Slight work! Easy money! You can walk. You can talk. Now just make it down these stairs without busting your ass, and you're golden, queen!

When I reach the top of the stairs, the song changes from something fast and a little rock to Taylor Swift's "Delicate"— not exactly a hype anthem, but I can make the vibes work for me. After taking another deep breath to calm my racing nerves, I place my bandaged hand on the rail and focus on steadying my feet with each step. Mel spots me from the other side of the dance floor. She waves and shouts, "Andie! You made it, you sexy bitch!"

I smile and wave back, somehow managing not to fumble my balance. I'm about halfway down when I notice Tommy waiting at the bottom of the steps. Waiting for me.

Has he been there this whole time?

I lock eyes with him just as my left ankle rolls to the

side. "Shit!" I mumble as I wobble, but I catch myself before I go down.

Tommy must read my lips, because now he's laughing and shaking his head. It's the particular laugh of his that makes his eyes crinkle at the sides and his smile stretch wide. His whole face lights up, and suddenly I feel warm. Now, even though I almost just completely bit it on the steps, I'm laughing a little bit too.

Before I take the final step, we come face-to-face, Tommy being almost a whole head taller than me. He reaches out a hand to help me down, but I can't exactly move just yet because he hasn't stepped back to give me room.

"Hi," I say.

"Hi," he says back, smiling.

We stand there long enough for me to take in the whole picture of him. His hair is different tonight. The usual messy waves that fall across his forehead and brows are brushed off to the side. It gives me a full view of the green eyes that like to stare and observe and judge and make you question things, both about him and yourself. He's got on a crisp white button-up shirt that's rolled at the sleeves and tucked into royal-blue dress pants. And he's wearing suspenders. Before I fully know what I'm doing, I reach out and gently tug at one of the suspenders. He looks down, and I can feel his warm breath brush against my hand.

"Hey. We match!" I say it the moment I realize it.

At this, he steps back, letting his eyes run up and down the length of me—the way they were while I was coming down the stairs. With his gaze all over me, I feel my cheeks warm.

"Look at us," he says. He raises his eyebrows and grins. "Like we planned it."

I finally take the last step. He turns his head as we both scan the dance floor and surrounding area. It's well past sunset, but everything is glowing with paper lanterns and string lights hanging overhead, and tea candles in mason jars on the tables. The party is casino-themed. Blackjack, roulette, and poker tables with professional dealers are scattered throughout for the adults, while the regular tables are topped with decks of cards and board games for everyone under twenty-one.

My eyes snag on his brother and Bekah, who are now sitting at a table on the edge of the dance floor. For a split second, Patrick and I make eye contact before he quickly looks away. I wonder how long he was looking at me standing here with Tommy.

"You ready?" Tommy asks.

"As I'll ever be," I say, exhaling long and slow. "You think he noticed my grand entrance?" I'm mainly asking as a joke, a way of lightening the heaviness that seems to have fallen over the space between us.

His eyes are unreadable when he says, "I think we all did."

My stomach does a little flip. I don't really know what to make of the feeling, so I decide to remind Tommy of *his* mission for the night. "And you figured out what you're gonna tell Chloe?" I ask, jabbing my index finger into his chest.

Tommy doesn't physically move away from my touch, but his eyes detach from mine. He just nods. "I think I did, yeah." he says.

"Okay, good," I say. "We'll both get our closure, and then we can enjoy the party?" I suggest, but it comes out at the same time he says . . .

"Do you want to dance first?"

I freeze. I wasn't expecting him to ask that. He reaches up to rub the back of his neck—a gesture he does a lot around me.

It takes me a moment to find words. Do I want to dance with Tommy? Why wouldn't I? He's my friend. I dance with Mel all the time. But why has that little flip turned into a Cirque du Soleil performance in my stomach?

"Sorry," I finally say, hoping my thoughts didn't play out across my face. "I've just been freaking out about this for a few days, and I kind of want to get past it," I explain. And that's the truth—at least part of it.

"For sure. For sure," he says. "I'll catch you after. You've got this."

Then he's gone before I can tell him I hope he's right.

Before I can get off the dance floor, the DJ strikes up "Uptown Funk," and instantly I'm surrounded. Tommy disappeared in a flash, and I'm about to go on the hunt for Patrick when two hands on my shoulders stop me from behind. Super-long metallic nails immediately clue me in that it's Mel. I turn and find her there in a sparkly red minidress that shows off her long tan legs. Her hair is slicked back into a low ponytail, and she's got silver stars on her cheeks and a bright red lip, making her look like a firecracker in human form.

"You look hot!" I tell her, spinning her around. "Where's Augie?" I ask when we're face-to-face again.

"Potty break."

I nod, and we start to dance on instinct as I not so subtly dart my head around, trying to spot Patrick.

"What's up?" Mel asks, obviously catching on to my weirdness. "You look like you're trying to evade the police. Should I be concerned?"

I lean in closer to her so she can hear me over the music without everyone around us hearing me over the music. "I'm trying to find Patrick."

"Huh?" She pulls back with her eyebrows wrinkled. I can tell there's no way she heard me over Bruno.

I try again. This time, I lean in farther and speak slower *and* louder. "I'm trying to find *Patrick*!"

And that's when the music stops.

There's practically complete silence just when my shouting Patrick's name echoes out around us, catching the attention of everyone in a twenty-foot radius—*including* Patrick and Bekah—who I hadn't realized were dancing about three feet to our left. Now they're both giving me looks while the DJ struggles to start the song back up. A chorus of mountain crickets and the rush of blood in my ears are the only soundtrack for this cursed moment.

There's a piercingly sharp burst of feedback before the DJ murmurs into the mic, "Sorry, guys. We'll get back to groovin' as soon as I find the cable that got kicked loose."

Mel and I stare at each other blankly. I sputter out

unintelligible sounds, trying to find a cover as Patrick starts to turn red.

"Mel!" Mrs. Bridges's voice cuts through the terrible absence of sound. "Drink down on the dance floor! Can you get the mop?"

Mel cringes and moves toward her mom. "Sorry," she whispers as I'm currently dying inside. "Don't think my parents insured the party. Bold choice, right?"

I'm standing by myself when the music starts back up. And this time it's something old and soulful, "Stand by Me." The partygoers all turn back to their dance partners and begin to sway.

There's nothing like a classic ballad about undying love to make a girl who's standing solo—right after shouting the name of her now-taken former crush for the whole world to hear—feel like a total loser.

I push out of the center of the dance floor but, against my better judgment, turn for one last look at Patrick and Bekah. I expect to see them gazing longingly into each other's eyes. Maybe he'll be playing with her hair or he'll be laughing at something she just said. Like I need the torture. But instead they're fully kissing—like models in a music video. I don't know how long I stare, but I catch myself, hopefully, before anyone notices, and turn quickly to leave the floor.

That's when I feel my foot slip on another wet spot.

My feet start to slide out from under me in slow motion. At this point, my only options are to crash-land on my tailbone or grab on to Mr. Rawcliffe's white chinos and risk pantsing him in public. In a split-second decision, I give up and accept my fate, but out of nowhere, a strong arm scoops around my waist from behind, and suddenly I'm lifted up to stand. When I turn around, I'm smacked with the full force of two green eyes.

"I leave you for five minutes, and the party descends into chaos," Tommy says with a laugh, his hands still resting on my hips.

Blame it on the rush of relief at the save, or maybe it's from seeing his freshly shaved face. But suddenly I'm throwing my arms around him. I bury my face in his chest and inhale deeply, waiting for my heart rate to slow.

I pull back, and without even really deciding to, we end up pressed close and dancing slow like all the couples around us. It happens so fast, I bet my *almost* fall was barely noticed by anyone but us. How *did* he manage that?

I can feel the warmth from Tommy's hands pressed to my lower back as I bring mine to rest high up on his shoulders. Clearing my throat, I say, "You know me. Drama's kind of my shadow these days. It follows me around like a pet."

We laugh for a second, and then his eyebrows draw flat. "I take it talking to my brother didn't go so well?"

I shake my head. I don't say that now that we're dancing,

talking to Patrick doesn't feel so urgent anymore. Maybe it can wait. "How about you? You text Chloe back?"

"Not yet," he admits. "Figure I'll save it for the fireworks." Just as the song reaches the part about mountains crumbling to the sea, Tommy takes my right hand with his left and steps back to spin me around. He twirls me in a circle, then brings both hands down to catch me at my waist before pulling us back into a slow two-step that's perfectly timed to the lazy melody.

"When did you learn to dance like this, Tommy Ling?" I ask him, truly shocked.

A dimple sinks deep into his left cheek when I say his full name. "My mom always likes to play old records at night after dinner," he tells me. "And sometimes when Dad's busy up in his office finishing work, she makes me her dance partner. We've been doing it since I was probably . . ." He pauses, looking up at the stars like he's counting the years. "Gotta be since I was nine or ten."

I'm about to tell him that he's full of surprises. And that I'm wondering what I'll find out next. But the song switches to something fast and bouncy and *super* retro. Mel's mom shouts, "Oh yeah! ABBA, baby! That's my jam!" Almost instantaneously everyone over the age of thirty crowds the dance floor.

"Think that's your cue," Tommy says. When I stare at him like he's just challenged me to a dance-off, he nods toward

Patrick and Bekah, who are headed back to their table. "If at first you don't succeed . . . ," he reminds me.

Oh, right. My Talk with Patrick. Stepping out of his arms, I take in a deep breath. "How do I look?" I ask, and his eyes go wide. "Never mind. Don't answer that," I cut in, realizing how awkward I've just made things.

"You got this, Andie Weaver," he says. "Just watch out for the spills."

And then I'm off. Again.

I was hoping to snag Patrick at a moment when he was alone. But apparently these two are glued at the hip. I bet she even goes with him to the restroom.

Walking up to their table is an out-of-body experience. Sort of how I imagine it might feel marching down the aisle of a packed church with plans to object to a wedding. Maybe I'm being a little dramatic. But busting up a flirt session between last year's crush and his current girlfriend to have a *Sorry I ghosted you. Can we still be friends?* conversation *is* a bit dramatic.

It doesn't help that they look *so* in love. Bekah's got her legs crossed and tangled up in Patrick's. His hands are grazing her outer thighs. Their faces are close, so close, they could kiss at any moment. To top it all off, she's playing with his hair. I might as well be housekeeping services showing up to sweep around their honeymoon suite—while they're still in bed.

But I've already stepped off the dance floor and entered their line of sight, so I can't really turn back now. Plus, I've got an audience. Mel, Augie, and Tommy are posted up at a table on the other side of the party. Everyone's shooting me thumbs-ups—well, everyone but Tommy. He just lifts his drink, giving me a *Good luck* nod like I'm up to bat at the bottom of the ninth inning with a tied game.

Patrick and Bekah must sense me coming close, because when I'm a few feet away, they turn and lock eyes with me like two deer in headlights. Immediately Patrick pulls up from their pretzel formation to lean against the back of his gold Chiavari chair. Bekah doesn't budge, keeping her legs interlocked with his. She aims a dazzling smile my way, teeth pearly white and gleaming. Patrick looks more like he's two seconds from becoming roadkill.

"Hey, guys," I say, trying to sound casual and unbothered—the opposite of how I feel. Like I practiced a hundred times alone in my room. "Fun party, huh?" I lift my hand to flick my hair before remembering that it's up in a bun.

"Yeah, it's great," Bekah says, surprising me again with her raspy, sexy voice.

Dammit, I forgot to adjust for that. I clear my throat to see if I can manage a lower key. "So, um, ahem . . . I was wondering if I could talk to Patrick. It'll only take a minute."

I look at them, mainly trying to get a read on Patrick's reaction. His neck muscles tense as he swallows. He glances over at Bekah, whose smile hasn't moved an inch. "You mind if I go with Andie for a sec, babe?" he asks.

She tilts her head, sipping from her straw and smiling at him sweetly. "All good with me," she says, tossing her long hair over her shoulder.

Patrick slowly stands to walk with me over to the fire pits.

Now that I've successfully completed the first part of my mission, extracting my target from his partner so we can have the Talk, it's time for the hard part—having the *actual* talk. After walking several paces in awkward silence, it's painfully obvious that I have completely forgotten how it feels to be Patrick Ling's friend. How, only a year ago, he was one of the easiest people in the world for me to talk to—besides Mel, of course. And how something so small as a botched first kiss changed *everything* between us.

"You okay?" Patrick asks, crash-landing into my depressive spiral. "Do you need me to get you some water?"

"Who, me?" I ask, looking to see if someone else joined us out of nowhere. "What do you mean?"

"Nothing," he says, shrugging. "It's just, your voice sounded kind of weird back there for a sec."

Totally busted, I cough and rub my throat. "Seasonal allergies," I lie, hoping to play it off.

"Really?" he asks, eyebrow quirking upward. "If you want, we can find my mom. She's always got Zyrtec in her bag and—"

"Patrick," I cut him off, because we are getting really sidetracked and I told Bekah this wouldn't take long. We've just reached the fire pits, and I'd like to get started before I chicken out completely. "I'm good, really. See, all better," I insist in my normal, *unsexy* voice.

We sit down with enough space for Big Bird to fit between us, and I'm preparing to launch into my opening remarks, when Patrick beats me to the punch. "Uhhh, so I'm actually glad we're finally talking," he starts, eyes shifting from my face to the flames. "I should have never kissed you last summer, Andie. It messed up our friendship, and I'm sorry."

I planned to be organized with my thoughts. I even prepared bullets. An agenda! I was going to first apologize for freaking out after we kissed last summer and explain that I disappeared out of sheer emotional immaturity and humiliation. Then I'd make the case for us being friends again, even though he's seeing someone. Because that little crush I had? Gone! A thing of the past. All those years of growing *feelings*? Zapped into thin air with the regular passage of space and time! This summer's Andie Weaver is different. She's mature. *Evolved.* Over it. Who knows, maybe this summer's Andie and Bekah can be friends too. Maybe we have things in common. Does she play soccer? Write smutty fic with her bestie? Thrift with her mom? Do the *NYT* crossword with her dad? If not, I'm sure there's *something* we could bond over!

I didn't expect Patrick to open with such a blow to my

ego. I mean, I was there. I know the kiss was a fail. But if I remember correctly, it was pretty good until we got so dis-gustingly interrupted.

"Patrick, it's okay," I tell him, trying to measure my response. Because I don't regret our kiss so much as I regret the way I acted after it. "We both had feelings we wanted to explore. It didn't work out for us. But there's no need for you to be sorry that we tried. *I'm* not."

Patrick looks at me with a furrowed brow and twists his lips.

We sit in silence for a beat, and my confusion grows. "What?" I ask. "I feel like I'm missing something."

"Evan never told you?" he asks, speaking slowly. "I thought that was why you ghosted."

I shake my head, and his drops low. A pit forms in my stomach. "Patrick, what are you talking about?"

"Andie, I kissed you on the beach last summer because . . ." He stops and winces, like it physically pains him to say this. "Evan kind of set it up. All summer the guys had been saying it was 'about time' we go for it. Of course I was curious about us. But mostly I gave in to the pressure."

I can hardly see or think past the blur of shock and embarrassment that's taking over my body. But somehow I find words. "Was . . . ," I say, choking back angry tears. "Was T-Tommy in on it too?"

"Tommy had no idea," Patrick insists. His hands dart out

to touch me, but at the last second, he draws them back.

Relief washes over me. The Tommy Ling I know by now wouldn't set me up like this. But I didn't think the Patrick I knew could either.

"And Maisy?" I ask.

"She was only supposed to come over if I signaled to Evan that I needed an interruption," Patrick confesses. By the sour look on his face, I can tell he's not proud. "I swear, Andie. I never gave the signal. She got loose and found that fish all on her own."

I could cry rivers. But instead I sit completely still staring at the fire pit's flames, contemplating launching myself into them.

"Andie." Patrick says my name so quietly. "I'm really sorry. I thought you knew this, that someone told you, and that's why you never responded when I messaged you asking if we could talk about it. I was going to tell you then. And I'm only telling you now because it's been eating at me all year."

Ignoring the part about how much keeping this secret has made *him* suffer, I tell him, "I never responded because . . ." I pause and take a deep breath, readying myself for the plunge. "I thought I was in love with you for three summers in a row. Then I finally had my chance to kiss you, got fish guts dumped in my lap in front of all our friends, and ran off into the lake to rinse myself off and keep from puking. I was *embarrassed*, Patrick. So embarrassed that I felt frozen by it."

"Andie, I'm sorry," he says again, eyes watery. Like this confession didn't bring the weightlessness he'd hoped it would.

"Yeah, you said that already," I tell him flatly.

A gunshot goes off in the distance, and it might as well have hit me in the chest. Except it wasn't a gunshot. It was a firework. It is the Fourth of July, after all. And as vibrant colors and shooting lights flood the sky, I can't sit here and look at Patrick looking at me the way he is now. Because his eyes are saying he's sorry again—which, as far as I'm concerned, is one of the emptiest words of the English language. So, I stand up and I bolt.

He calls after me, but I don't turn back.

CHAPTER EIGHTEEN

"You'd better go get our girl." Mel leans into my shoulder to shout above the sound of the fireworks show.

Andie is a sparkly flash of blue darting across the lawn from the fire pit where she was just sitting and talking with Patrick. I already know where she's heading. I lock gazes with Mel, nod once, and dart off in the same direction at a fast pace.

I'm halfway across the lawn, taking long strides and realizing that Andie's a winger on her varsity team for good reason, when Patrick jogs up to catch me. "Hey, bro!" he calls.

Everything in me wants to pretend I didn't hear him.

With Roman candles soaring loud and bright over us, I could *almost* get away with it too. But I make a split-second decision to stop in my tracks and see what he's got to say.

"Sup, man?" I ask, trying to mask the fact that I'm in a rush and slightly annoyed by the interruption.

He makes a subtle nod in the direction Andie ran off to. "You going after her?"

I stuff my hands into my pockets and nod. "Yeah. Was gonna see if she needs anything."

Patrick's eyebrows scrunch, and he looks at me without blinking. "Is something going on between you two?" There's no accusation in the question, just genuine curiosity.

I spend all of two seconds figuring out what I'm going to say. What ends up coming out is as much truth as I can manage out of the current state of my jumbled-up feelings. "She needs a friend. I'm just trying to be that."

Patrick eyes me for a few long seconds without saying anything, like he's trying to get an honest read. I'm anxious to get to Andie, to see how things went from her perspective.

This is a strange feeling, being sized up by my little brother. At the same time, I think I like that he's being a bit protective of her right now. I know she says she's heartbroken over Patrick, but I feel like it's this being in limbo over their friendship that's done the most damage.

Patrick nods, like in those seconds of silence he made

some kind of private decision about me. "She's probably heading for the dock," he says, pointing over my shoulder.

I nod back and clap him on the shoulder, not bothering to say that that's where I was already going.

Patrick turns to head back into the party, and I break into a jog to catch up to her.

Andie stands at the end of the dock looking up at the fireworks finale, the greens, reds, purples, and blues in the sky reflecting off the shimmery fabric of her blue dress.

Because of the show up above, she can't hear or even feel me walk up behind her. And even when I step up to her side, she doesn't show any signs of noticing I'm here. I can only tell she's aware of having company when she leans into my side to rest her head on my shoulder. I breathe in the peachy, vanilla scent of her shampoo. I first noticed it earlier while we were dancing. The same way I noticed how much I liked being close enough to smell her hair and feel the curls that escaped her bun tickle my face. How having my hands on her waist and hers on my neck gave me chills. How the reality of being with Andie in those moments made me want to completely scrap tonight's mission of texting Chloe back altogether. And how none of this is part of what we agreed on with our deal for the summer.

Even now, I don't know if I should wrap my arm around her or grab her hand and interlock our fingers.

Both options seem more wrong than right in this moment. So I settle for just planting my feet and being a sturdy post for her to lean into.

I can tell that her talk with Pat didn't go well. Not only from the way she literally ran off from him but also from the look in my brother's eyes when he stopped me as I went after her. I was *literally* in the middle—exactly where I don't want to be. But here on the dock with Andie, I don't want to be anywhere else.

For a long while we just stand in silence taking it all in. Then, suddenly, we're staring at a sky full of smoke, our ears still ringing from the pops and bangs of the finale. The DJ starts up another set in the distance.

With a mind of its own, my arm wraps around her shoulders for comfort. I know it was the right thing to do when she sinks further into my side. If only I could figure out the right thing to say.

"Tommy?" she asks.

"Mm-hmm?" I say back, swallowing thickly.

"Will you tell me about your book? Tell me about the star-crossed lovers?" she asks, and in this moment, I can't imagine denying her.

I clear my throat, because I was not expecting this at all. "Ahem . . . Sonam and Maxis—"

"I like those names," she says, and I can hear the smile on her voice.

"Thanks," I say, happy that this seems to be a solid distraction. "They're both seventeen and they've known each other since birth. Their mothers were best friends who grew up in a village called Everleah."

"Ah, a friends-to-lovers story." She sighs. "That's a great trope."

I chuckle. "Well, they started out as enemies—"

"Even better."

"But one day at the trading post, Sonam nearly gets kidnapped by Heir-class traffickers. That's the ruling class," I say to clarify. "Sonam has a natural beauty that's rare in the Feral Lands, and the king's guardsmen have had their eyes on her for a long time. But Maxis rescues her by posing as a member of the king's guard and stealing her away before she's shackled."

"Maxis is a badass, eh?" Andie says, and her voice sounds more normal now. Less like she could cry at any moment.

"Yeah," I say. "But mostly he's just in love."

She hums. "That's nice."

"So anyway," I continue, "after that, Sonam asks why Maxis would risk his life to save her, and he admits he's loved her since they were eight and she threw rocks at the kids who bullied him for his stutter. They kiss for the first time. But now Sonam has to live in hiding until they can both escape and build a life together far away from the Feral Lands."

"Tommy?" Andie says.

"Yeah?"

"I'm really into this story," she says. "I meant it when I said I want to read everything you've written."

For a beat, I don't say anything. Because as much as I've enjoyed talking to her about the world I've created, I think she needs to get some things off her chest.

"Tell me how things went with Patrick," I say. "If you want to."

"Oh, he basically confirmed what I already knew," she says, her voice wobbly again. "That every time he looks at me—" She stops to take a breath. "He sees dead fish."

When I don't laugh, she elbows me in the side. "Come on! You know that was a good one."

"Yeah, yeah," I give in. "But for real," I say, trying to be serious.

She takes a deep breath. "Basically," she says, "he thinks I ghosted him because I found out he only kissed me because Evan egged him on. He's very sorry and regrets the whole thing."

I didn't expect this revelation, and now I'm seeing red. A good part of me wants to run off to find Evan and my brother right this second, but I look down and notice a single tear that falls from Andie's right eye and realize that my time would be better spent right here. I can deal with them later. I reach up to catch her tear with my thumb. She cups her cheek where I just touched her.

"And how do you feel about it right this second?" I ask her.

"Like I officially lost a friend tonight," she admits, snorting. "Like a fool who thought she was falling for that friend last year, when all she really fell for was a prank."

I wrap my arm tighter around her shoulders. We stand there in the kind of silence that you rack your brain trying to find the right words to fill. Finally I give up and just rub my fingers back and forth over her bare shoulder—hoping my touch offers the comfort my words can't.

Eventually she breaks the quiet. "Okay, well. Enough about me," she says, sniffing back her tears. She steps out of my hold. "If we don't stop talking about this, I'm jumping into the lake and ruining this dress," she insists. "How did things go with Chloe?" She's wiping the wetness from her face now, and whatever small string that pulled between us a second ago feels like it's just snapped.

The last thing I want to do is change the subject right now, but it's probably best to just follow her lead. She's already dealt with enough *big* emotions tonight, and clearly she wants a distraction. So I make the quick adjustment. "Ahem . . . It went . . ." I rub the back of my neck. "It was good."

She squints at me, like she's not convinced.

"It was!" I insist. "I . . . wished her a happy Independence Day."

Andie stares at me blankly. "And?"

"And I told her I hoped she was having a good summer . . ."

I trail off when I realize I don't actually want to tell her how the rest of the conversation went. I'm not exactly sure why, either. It is part of our deal, after all.

"That all sounds really nice, Tommy," Andie says as her eyes narrow. "But I feel like you're not telling me something." She crosses her arms, and I make myself not look down at what that does to her chest.

She's right, anyway. For some reason I *am* holding back. I feel like a bug squirming under her magnifying glass. Maybe Andie is invested in me just as much as I'm invested in her. Maybe we're both in a little deeper than we bargained for. I breathe in and out, slow and steady. "She told me she misses me."

Andie's eyes widen. "She said that exactly? She said, *Tommy, I miss you?*"

I nod without breaking eye contact.

Andie swallows, and the breeze from the lake rustles the loose curls around her face. "And what did you say?" she asks.

"I told her I miss her too," I admit with a shrug. Because it's the truth. But not as true as it was two weeks ago. Or even two hours ago. But that's the part I'll keep to myself, because I don't know what good admitting it out loud right now will do. Tonight's deal was about us getting clarity, not opening up a can of radioactive worms. Plus, she's just finished wiping away tears over Patrick's asshat behavior. She needs a friend right now. Not more confusion.

Andie nods. Her eyes are glassy when she turns to look at the water. She's noticeably less enthusiastic about this Chloe update than she was about the last one. Is that because tonight has put her through the ringer, or for *other* reasons?

"I'm sorry, Tommy," she says, blowing air through her lips. "I don't mean to take it out on you. It's just been a shitty night for me and I'm having a hard time rallying."

"We can sit," I suggest. "If it won't ruin your dress."

She hikes up her skirt and sits down without a care in the world for the fate of her dress. "I thought you'd never ask." She sighs.

I plop down on the dock next to her while she undoes her heels. I force myself to look away, but only after I make a mental note of how the gold straps perfectly contrast with her smooth brown skin. Behind us, the DJ starts playing a SZA song about life on Saturn and breaking patterns, and the smoke in the sky is nearly faded enough for us see the stars.

"If you lost a friend tonight," I tell her, "count me in as a new one."

"You mean to tell me you're just my friend as of tonight?" she asks, eyebrows shooting up.

"I don't know." I shrug and look up at the moon, really playing it up. "You've been calling me your emotional-support gerbil or whatever. I'm just tryna get an upgrade."

She laughs, and it's a full-throated, head-falling-back kind of laugh that makes me feel like I just scored a home run.

CHAPTER NINETEEN

In the three days since the Fourth of July, steady rain has soaked the mountain and almost overflowed the lake. Our house is waterlogged, and the sky's been dark and dreary. It's all very fitting, given the vibes me and Mom have been trading since the party. Looks like we both struck out on Independence Day, because things went about as well with her and Tawny Bridges's tech guy as they did with me and Patrick. Mom even had to block him after he sent her an unsolicited dick pic while we were in the middle of eating at the Old German Deli.

She's at the kitchen sink now, filling in my Aunt Sheila

on all the gory details. "I just never thought I'd be *here* again. Or . . . ever, to be honest . . . ," she laments over a sink of soapy dishes.

Aunt Sheila lives with her family all the way in New York, but she and my mom are still super close. In previous years, she and her husband, my Uncle Devin, would bring my cousins Malik and Sybil out to the lake house for big family gatherings for the holidays. This summer, they're all spending time on Martha's Vineyard with Devin's parents, so Mom has to settle for catching up over the phone.

"You know, *dating* again," she explains to Aunt Sheila. "I thought for sure that with David, I was out of the game for good. But now with all this swiping left and right, I swear it's giving me carpal tunnel. And don't get me started on the sexting. I never asked to see so many penises. I was perfectly content with just the one."

"Girl, I know," I can hear Aunt Sheila say over the speakerphone. "If Devin dies, or we call it quits, I'm taking a vow of celibacy. Mark my words. I'll be *done*. Dating was hard enough *before* I had to do it with cellulite."

Mom's laugh turns into a tired sigh. "So, there's something I've been meaning to tell you." Her voice slips low as her eyes quickly dart up to where they catch hold of mine.

Whoops! I thought I was being slick. Had my earbuds in without any music playing while *pretending* to be in my own little world, journaling at the kitchen island.

But now that I've been busted snooping, Mom winks at me and heads for the sliding glass door that leads out to the covered patio. The remnants of her conversation with my aunt fade away with the sound of the rain as she slides the door closed behind her. I would bet a million dollars I don't have that right now she's telling Aunt Sheila about the Letter.

Naturally I grab my phone and start tapping away.

Me: Mom's telling Aunt Sheila about the Letter RIGHT NOW

Mel: OMG

Mel: Are you taking notes?????

Me: She went outside. Can't hear shit!

Mel: Oh! And! Augie wasn't in on it!

Mel: Which thank god bc I would have dropped him like Calc BC

Me: What r u talking about?!

Mel: omg the kiss! Maisy! The fish! Patrick's betrayal!

Mel: Augie swore on Grandma Lucy he was today years old when he found out

Me: Anybody do a welfare check on Grandma Lucy?

Mel: I believe him babe ♥

Me: I know. Me too.

It's true. Augie may be *a lot* of things—loud, oblivious, gassy with no shame. But a liar he is not.

Mel: I can tell ur moping. Stop it! Come to the movies with us!

Mel: U can bring Tommy

Me: Why would I do that?

Mel: Uhhh cuz ur friends

Mel: And u like him

My face heats when this text comes through.

Me: I do NOT like him

Mel: I don't mean it like that! But he's cool right?

Mel: riiiiigghttttt?

Me: Yeah. He's cool

I breathe a sigh of relief. Maybe Mel wasn't suggesting something deeper going on between me and Tommy. Because even if he looked really good in those suspenders at the party—and even if it felt really good to slow dance with him, and to rest my head on his very strong shoulder as he casually massaged my arm during the fireworks—it's clear that he and Chloe are on their way toward getting back together. *And* he's Patrick's brother. I may be a hot mess, but I'm not *messy*.

But despite all that, Tommy *is* my friend. I know this to be true. He said as much when he came to my rescue before I even needed to send an SOS. We've got a good rhythm going, the two of us, and we're not in danger of kissing and ruining things. So I don't have to overthink this. I tap out a response to Mel: Ok ill ask him

Me: Hey wyd?

Tommy: I am a creature of habit. Writing. U?

Me: About to go to the movies. Augie's driving, u wanna come?

Tommy: sure. Be on ur porch in 5

Me: k. but before u come over, send me the last chapter u wrote

Me: pretty pleeeeaaaaseeee

Tommy: what's ur email?

Me: 😵

Me: andie.weaver@sunmail.com

Tommy: sent

Me: I could get used to this

Tommy: don't 😉

"That movie kinda sucked," Augie says, before stretching his arms wide with a yawn.

The four of us are walking out of the movie theater on Pine Knot Ave. It's a little after seven at night, and the dark clouds have parted just in time to let the sunset have its moment. The reds, oranges, and yellows of the vibrant sky reflect off the wet asphalt of the parking lot, and dampness clings in the air.

"To be fair, babe," Mel says, wrapping an arm around his waist, "you *were* snoring through at least half of it. So you're technically disqualified from giving a critique."

"And," I jump in, hiding my laughter, "you *did* talk through the first half."

Augie looks truly wounded, with his mouth dropping into a wide O shape.

Tommy, who's walking between the two of us, says, "It's okay, man." He pats him hard on the back. "Your snores kept me awake through that mushroom dream sequence." He turns his head to me and moves his eyebrows up and down.

"Yeah," I say, playing along. "If you hadn't pissed off the snooty millennials behind us, I would have been comfy enough to doze off too. Then I would have missed that whole part with the floating babies in outer space."

"Oh! I think I missed that when I went to the restroom," Mel says from Augie's other side. "Was it before or after they hitchhiked to Alaska and got abducted by the circus clowns?"

Augie stops short, bringing us all to a halt. "Wait, what the hell are you guys talking about?" He looks genuinely bewildered.

After a few seconds of silence, the three of us burst into laughter.

A beat later, Augie catches on. "Okay, Tommy-Boy! You're the ringleader of this," he says. "And for that, pizza's on you."

Augie's Jeep is parked at the end of a long row of cars. He and Mel are holding hands as we make our way through the lot. It's unseasonably cold tonight, and as we walk, I wrap my arms around my waist to keep myself from shivering.

"I've got you," Tommy says, his low, grumbly voice making me shiver even more. He wraps an arm around my shoulders and pulls me close. Instantly I'm warm and breathing in his scent of oranges and pine trees. He smells so good, I can't stop myself from leaning in for a full whiff. I'm smiling until I catch

Mel's bug-eyed stare—like she's just caught me shoplifting.

She smirks and mouths, *I knew it!* Rolling my eyes, I turn away, pretending I saw and did nothing objectionable. Because what? Can't a girl admire a boy who smells nice every now and then?

I know Mel's onto me. Truth is, I'm onto myself. I like Tommy Ling. But I won't let myself like him *too* much. Not after the Fourth of July reveal that he told Chloe he misses her. And not after finding out that the last time I let myself fall for a Ling brother, I walked into a trap of humiliation.

Still, I want to be around him. Lounging on the dock figuring out life, talking about books. Even sitting in dark theaters watching weird movies and clocking every time he laughs. If this is my last summer at the lake like this, I'm glad Tommy Ling gets to be such a huge part of it.

I feel the sudden urge to take a mental picture of the four of us walking through the parking lot right now. Because who knows if we'll all be back at the lake next summer? After high school, Mel's planning to move across the country to study design at SCAD. Augie's going to take a gap year to work flipping houses at his dad's contracting business. And Tommy could either be on a team with the minor leagues or at UCLA crafting the next great American novel. If all goes to plan, I'll have a soccer scholarship at Stanford. And maybe we'll all be so busy in our own corners of the world that we won't have time to return to this one.

After pizza, Augie brings me home before dropping Tommy off next door at his house. I know something's off the moment they all drive away.

My first sign is the second car—marked RENTAL—in the driveway when I walk up to the porch. Then it's the extra set of keys in the bowl at the entry when I drop my tote there. But a mug of tea sitting half-full on the kitchen counter gives it away completely. Because it isn't just any mug.

It's *his* mug.

I pull out my earbuds, whipping my head around to check for more signs that my dad is, or was, here. My stomach sinks. Because we've been keeping the Ring a secret from my mom for weeks. He told me he'd find the time to tell her "in person," but he didn't give me a heads-up that it would be now. Even though Tawny Bridges's matchmaking plans weren't all that successful, Mom really came out of her shell on the Fourth of July. She played blackjack. Got tipsy. Even went full-out to "Get Me Bodied" on the dance floor. Her spark came back, and I was hoping it was here to stay.

When I hear voices on the patio, I look through the kitchen-sink window and spot them. Mom is pacing while Dad talks with big hand gestures. They've got the familiar strained, tight expressions that marked the last couple of years of every disagreement I saw them have.

I quickly reach into my pocket to turn off the music that's

still blasting from my phone. The window is open, with only the screen separating the inside from out. And without my playlist going, I can hear everything clearly.

"V," Dad says. His voice is tired but pleading. My chest pulls at the center. Even though I'm used to this, I hate it when they fight. "You never gave me a chance to handle the truth. And *that* was the problem."

"David, I'm sorry. But we've been over this," Mom pleads with him too. "If I could go back—if I knew it would come to *this* . . . I would have told you everything twenty years ago."

"You let me be cordial with him, V. Go fishing! Smoke cigars!" Dad says, his words slicing through the damp air like blades. "And all that time I had no idea he loved you first. Do you know how foolish that makes me?"

"He wasn't *in love* with me, David," Mom says. "It was our past. It wasn't supposed to dictate our future."

My heart is in my throat. Because I think what I'm hearing is that my mom hid things from my dad, maybe even cheated on him and lied to me about it. If any of this is true, I'm not sure Mom's arguments are all that convincing. And I can tell by the way my dad is shaking his head that he's not buying any of it either.

"If I couldn't trust you to be honest with me about this, how can I trust that you've been honest with me at all? About anything? What kind of marriage was that, V?"

"David, apart from this, I have *never* kept a thing from

you. And you know we had other problems. *Real* problems."
Mom's voice cracks. With it, something inside me cracks too.
I hate seeing him so angry and her so exhausted. I hate see-
ing the ugly, messy parts of love, especially from my parents.
"I asked you to come to counseling with me for yea—"

"V, there was no point in that," Dad says, cutting her off.
"Therapy wasn't going to fix us."

This is the moment when I can see my mom give up the
fight. No more pleading or convincing. I've seen it so many
times between the two of them. Dad being stubborn. Mom
letting go so easily.

"Then why did you come here, David?" Mom asks, her
shoulders sinking. "The papers are signed. We've already
started rebuilding our lives. Andie's just getting adjusted to
this new version of us. Why come up here and start this now?"

Dad hesitates, drops his head. "Because I met someone,"
he says, and it's barely above a whisper but still loud enough
for me to hear.

Mom stops pacing. A short huff of humorless laughter
falls from her lips. "I'm aware that you have a girlfriend,
David. So is all of Instagram," she says. Then she cocks her
head to the side. "David, are you getting married?"

When Mom asks this, Dad just stands and stares at her
for what feels like an entire minute. "I'm proposing to her
next week."

Clunk!

It takes a second for me to realize that the noise came from me. I just dropped my water bottle into the sink, and the clanging sound could probably be heard on the other side of the lake. When both of my parents' faces turn toward me lurking in the kitchen window, it's painfully clear that this is not a reality show. It's my mess of a family.

I spin and bolt from the kitchen. Apparently, I'm great at getaways. Ten years of competitive soccer have got to be good for something. Except, in doing so, I accidentally knock into my dad's mug and send it crashing to the floor. I'm not sure if it breaks into a thousand pieces, because I don't turn back to see.

They can pick up their mess. I'm heading for the dock.

THIRTY MINUTES EARLIER

After we grabbed a bite at Saucy Mama's Pizzeria, where Augie challenged me to an arm-wrestling match and quickly lost twenty bucks, I get home on a high. Maybe getting out of my head and into the world is good for me every now and then. But after a day's worth of doing just that, I'm ready to jump back into my manuscript.

Due to her persistence, I've sent Andie some chapters I'm stuck on, and she's been giving me her thoughts. Like last night, when I woke up at one a.m. to vibrations under my pillow.

Andie: Dude.

Tommy: yes?

Andie: This is great but why so dark? Why did Sonam's mom and sister BOTH have to die?

Tommy: because

Tommy: issa tragedy

Tommy: u know . . . like Hamlet

Andie: pretty sure that's a trage-comedy

Andie: And what if just the mom dies? Let sis live and give Sonam somebody to come back and fight for.

Andie: Somebody other than Maxis I mean

Andie: but that's just my 2 cents

Tommy: ah so we upgraded from a penny

Andie: genius comes at a price these days #inflation

Tommy: u have given me something to think about now srsly go to bed

Andie: night night

Tommy: good night

Between Andie's notes and the weird movie we just saw, I think I've got enough inspiration for an all-night writing session. Augie was right, the movie did kind of suck. But I sort of liked the way it didn't seem to know, or care, about genre conventions. I may have told Andie I'm writing a dystopian romance—that has since veered toward a tragic love story. But that's because it's the easiest way to sum up the concept in a few words. And the more I think about it, I'm really just letting this story and its characters dictate what they'll become based on how I feel. I can leave it up to readers to decide what labels to put on it.

After walking past the kitchen, I stop and decide to make a visit to the fridge for some creative fuel—that's two Snapples, a bag of carrots, and some hummus, plus a sleeve of Oreos from the cabinet. It should be enough to keep me going for a while.

When all the snacks are meticulously balanced between my arms and chin, I kick the fridge door closed before jumping almost two feet in the air at the shock of seeing my dad standing an inch from my face on the other side of it. He didn't say *Boo!* but he might as well have, by the way my heart rate skyrockets.

By some miracle, I manage to drop everything onto the countertop instead of the floor. "Holy shit, Dad! You could have given me a warning."

"Son," he says flatly, voice stern and eyes hard on mine. "Explain something to me," he says, very ominous. "How is it that Rick Ackerman—you know, the college teammate and minor-league scout I introduced you to—had you on his call sheet today to discuss a tryout but you were a no-show?"

When he finishes, he just stands there hovering, waiting for my response. Sizing me up like I'm eight years old again and getting busted for making a scavenger hunt out of his state-of-the-art power tools.

Just like back then, now I have absolutely nothing to say

for myself. I completely forgot about the call. I'd been writing when Andie's text about the movie came through. I jumped at the chance to go out with her, and the call with Rick Ackerman didn't even cross my mind after that.

"Dad, I'm sorry," I tell him, pinching the bridge of my nose. "Maybe I can reschedule for another ti—"

"Have a seat, son." He cuts me off before pulling out a stool. The scratch of the legs sliding on the tile floor sends a chill down my spine. Already, I know this is about to turn into a much larger conversation—one I've been expecting and dreading at the same time.

"Tommy, we both know you're not an irresponsible kid. You're in your head a lot, sure. But your mom and I know you're not a flake," Dad says, and I'm almost certain the compliments will end here. "So from that I gather that something else has got to be going on here. If I'm going to put my name and reputation on the line to try to get you a *second* chance with this scout, I need to know if it's worth the trouble."

Dad crosses his arms over his chest and waits me out.

I take my time answering him and let out a slow, shuddering breath. For months, I've known this moment was coming. My senior season was make or break, and our team won the state title. My scholarship coming through at UCLA is thanks in large part to how well I played. None of that makes what I'm about to say any easier, though. That I loved baseball for a long time, but I think it's served its purpose for me. And now maybe it's time for me to move on.

Just when I'm about to open my mouth to say it, Mom rounds the corner from the dining room. She walks up to Dad's side with a serious look on her face. And once again, I'm being double-teamed. It's probably for the best that they're both here to hear this. After all, they were both there at all the practices and games and camps, cheering me on all these years. It was both of them who poured their all into me and Patrick, and both of them who have these great expectations for my future with baseball. It's also both of them that I know I'll be letting down.

"Mom, Dad," I start, with my voice a little shaky. "First off, I'm sorry for missing the call with the scout. I have no excuse, and I'll email him tomorrow with an honest apology for wasting his time."

They look at each other, then back to me.

"Second, I need you both to know that I love and appreciate you for all the time and money and energy you've invested in me all these years. And, Dad, I'm really grateful you called in a favor with your old teammate. I know a lot of people in my position would kill to have the kind of support I do. And that's why it's been so hard for me to tell you this." I stop to take a breath.

"Tell us what, honey?" Patience has never been my mom's best quality. And with the way her brows are drawn together, you'd think she's worried that I'm about to admit to a felony.

I release my breath and let the truth out with it. "I don't want to go pro," I say, and instantly my chest feels lighter. Then I lay the heavier blow: "I don't even know if I want to play at all anymore."

At this, Dad's hands go up to scrub through his salt-and-pepper hair. Mom drops her head. In my mind, I've imagined this reaction shot over and over like an instant replay. And each time it went exactly like this—me crushing their hopes and dreams.

"Son, what do you *mean* you don't know?" Dad asks a few seconds after the shock of the bomb I just dropped wears off. Now his mouth is set into a rigid line. Mom, whose eyes are watery, puts a calming hand on his forearm, which is flexed hard on the countertop.

At this point, I am shrinking. I no longer feel like I'm eight. Now I'm the five-year-old confessing I crashed my tricycle into the flat-screen TV.

"I . . . I mean, maybe I just take a year off from baseball?" I suggest. "I figure that way I can see what I'm like without it? Maybe I'll find out what other things I'm good at in college."

Dad's up now, pacing in the small space between the fridge and the island. "And what about your scholarship, son? Did you think about how you're going to pay for college without baseball? Or better yet, *who's* going to pay for college?"

"Honey, let's take a beat," Mom says, jumping in now. She lays a hand on his back. "Maybe let's just hear him out."

"Hear him out?" he spits back. "He's a kid. He's got no idea what he wants!"

That sends a ball of fire shooting through my chest. All my life, I feel like they've made decisions for me. Planned it all out and just brought me and Patrick along for the ride. But here I am, basically an adult, finally telling them what I want, and I'm being completely dismissed. I'm so angry, the words fall out of me before I can think. "Dad, if you want an all-star to live out your dreams, you've still got Pat."

Dad's nostrils flare as he waves me off. "Pat doesn't have your arm, kid!"

By the horrified look on my mom's face, I can tell that we've got company without even turning around. When my dad's eyes dart to the side, just past mine, I know they crash right into my brother's—because of the instant remorse that fills them.

My fists clench so tight, I can feel the nails digging into my palms. *This* is what I've always tried to avoid. Comparison. I know our stats, and our playing styles. I've also heard the rumblings from the many coaches over the years who've projected that I could have a real shot at the pros, all the while making hedging comments about my brother. Worst of all, I know he's heard them too. But none of it has dampened his love for the game or his determination for us to play together in the league.

When I turn to my brother, the look on his face is one I've never seen before. "I . . . I just came down to get some drinks for me and Bekah," he says before swallowing hard. "I didn't mean to—"

"Pat," I say, unsure of what should come next. "I'm sorry, I—"

"Patrick and Tommy," my mother interjects, her voice clear and strong. "We're sorry, boys, for how this went. Now could you give your father and me the kitchen?"

We turn to them and nod. Then we get the hell out of the way.

CHAPTER TWENTY-ONE

On my way to the dock, I don't walk. I run. The drizzle has picked back up, but I don't mind. Something about the rain feels comforting to me now—like I'm not the only one crying, because the sky's doing it too.

My generation gets a bad rap these days. From my standpoint, the adults are the ones in a near-constant state of crashing out. Why would my dad drive all the way up here just to give my mom a hard time about the mistakes she made in their marriage, when he's about to propose to somebody else? And how can Mom expect Dad to so easily get over the fact that she spent years hiding something so obviously big from him?

Why can't people just say how they feel, when they feel it, before it's too late? Wouldn't that save us all from the drama?

By the time I reach the dock, the drizzle has dissipated to barely a mist. I can feel my phone vibrating in my pocket, and when I check the screen, it's Mom.

"Honey, where did you go?" she asks, her voice panicked. "We should really talk."

"Mom, it's okay," I tell her, so exhausted by the topic that I can hardly imagine talking about it now. "I'm just on the dock. I'm fine. I swear. Can we talk tomorrow?"

"It's raining, Andie," Mom says, as if I couldn't tell. "Your dad left. He's staying at a rental. He told me to apologize for surprising you like that. Will you *please* come back inside? I don't want you out there alone tonight."

In my peripheral vision, I catch a glimpse of someone coming down the dock as she's talking. Because of the mist, he's blurry in the distance. But I know exactly who he is.

"I'm not alone, Mom. I'm here with—" Thinking fast, I tell her, "Mel."

I hear a loud breath on the other end of the line before she says, "Okay, but you two get inside soon. And be home by midnight if you're not sleeping over there, okay? Text me when you're in bed. Promise?"

"I will, Mom," I tell her. "Promise."

"Okay. G'night, Andie-Bug. I love you."

"Night, Mom. Love you too."

Tommy's almost reached me at the end of the dock now, and before he does, I tap out a series of texts to Mel.

Me: If my mom asks, I'm with you on the dock

Mel: K.

Mel: But who are you really with?

Me: . . . Tommy

Mel: Right. Duh.

"You trying to catch a cold?" Tommy asks before handing me a blanket. He's in jogging pants and a T-shirt that's plastered to his chest from what's got to be sweat, because it's not raining that hard yet. He must have seen me on the dock while he was out for a run. Did he make a pit stop for the blanket?

I take the fleece wrap and throw it around my shoulders, making note of how he always seems to come prepared. First it was the cooler with snacks on the beach, and now this. He's a few feet away—not even close enough to touch—and still, him being here with just what I need, at exactly the right time, feels like being held.

"Thanks," I tell him. And then because part of me wants to know if he's a mind reader, I ask, "What are you doing out here?"

He shrugs. "I was out for a jog and got a feeling that maybe you'd need your heartbreak-support pig. Figured I'd find you out here."

I sniff and swipe at the unruly curls that are sticking to

my tearstained face. I know my voice is shaky, but oddly, I don't feel like I have to try to hide that in front of Tommy. "But I didn't send the SOS," I say. "And, what? You're some kind of shape-shifter now? I thought you were a gerbil."

He laughs and shakes his head. "When Augie dropped us off after pizza, I noticed the extra car at your house. Then I spotted your dad through a window. It didn't take all that much for me to put it together," he says. "Plus, pigs are supersmart. Gerbils are lame. I decided I wanted a rebrand."

"Okay, Mr. Pig, you should probably consider trying out for the FBI with those supersmart observation skills of yours," I tell him. I'm so relieved to be talking about something of absolutely zero importance that I almost forget what I was crying about.

"Anyway, you guessed right. This meltdown," I say, pointing at my sloppy face, "has nothing to do with Patrick and everything to do with the fact that my parents are an emotional train wreck. So you're off the hook for the night. Don't mind the tears. I'm fine. Great, actually!"

"Andie, you're obviously not fine," he says, and I try not to take offense. "It doesn't matter what it's about. If you need somebody, I can *be* that somebody."

Okay. That might be the simplest, sweetest thing anybody's ever said to me. Tommy Ling is good at this emotional-support thing.

"So . . . do you want to talk about it?" Tommy asks.

"Absolutely not," I answer.

His mouth tips up on one side, like he expected me to say just that. "Well, what do you want to do instead?"

I think for a second, chewing on my lip. Then I get an idea. "You ever seen this movie called *Never Been Kissed*?"

Sinking down into the plush couch in the Lings' basement movie room feels familiar and new at the same time. I can't count the days I've wasted playing video games and binging shows down here with Patrick. But tonight, for the first time, I'm here alone with Tommy. To top it off, I'm wearing his clothes—an oversize sweatshirt and a pair of shorts I've rolled twice at the waist to keep them from falling off. Of course they smell like him too, woodsy with a hint of soap—a definite upgrade from my rain-soaked jeans. And while he navigates the remote so we can stream the movie, I busy myself taking mental notes of him.

He's sitting about six inches away from me with a bowl of freshly popped popcorn and a package of dried-mango strips between us. He's wearing basketball shorts with a gray T-shirt, and his long legs and bare feet stretch to the end of the footrest. For a moment, I wonder what he'd do if I moved closer. If I moved the popcorn and the snacks and curled myself around his frame. But Mel would say, *Absolutely not. Never make the first move!*

Scolded by my thoughts, I force my focus back toward

the screen. Tommy presses play on the movie, then tosses a handful of popcorn into his mouth—completely normal, unbothered, and seemingly unaffected by my presence.

Within seconds, I'm no longer watching the movie because I'm watching him. The way the images dance across his irises, and the way the muscles of his jaw tense and loosen as he chews. Then my eyes drift down the length of him to where his forearms cradle the popcorn bowl on his lap. I reach over for some, thinking I'll distract myself with the warm, salty, buttery goodness. After taking a bite, I close my eyes and hum at how delicious it tastes. When I open them, Tommy's no longer looking at the movie either.

"That good, huh?" he asks with a small smirk and his eyes locked on mine.

Smiling, I say, "Mm-hmm," before reaching over to his lap and grabbing another handful. His eyes slowly track my movement.

"You cold?" he asks. The question comes out of left field, but now that I think of it, it does feel kind of chilly in here.

Expecting he'll go grab me a blanket, I nod and say, "Mm-hmm." I'm afraid if I say anything more, I'll confess that I'm crushing on him in a big way—something I've barely even confessed to *myself*. How else to explain the warm, gooey feeling that fills me when watching him doing something so simple as eating popcorn? And I don't think either of us is ready for that revelation.

Instead of getting up, he surprises me and sets the popcorn bowl to the side, closing the distance between us and tucking me into him. "Comfortable?" he asks.

"Mm-hmm," I repeat, and then quickly shove a handful of popcorn into my mouth. "So comfy," I mumble around the kernels. I can both hear and feel his laugh as it rumbles through his chest.

Minutes pass, and I have no idea what's happening on the screen. Probably because I'm busy counting each rise and fall of his chest and memorizing the rhythm of his heartbeats. He could reach over, lift my chin, and kiss me right now, and I would not object. Matter of fact, with a few adjustments, I could perfectly position myself to kiss him.

I don't know how long I spend analyzing the logistics of our potential kiss. Because within seconds of his fingers tracing lazy circles on my scalp, I'm falling fast asleep.

wake up to a vibrating pillow. After prying my eyes open, I check my phone and find a text from Andie. She fell asleep on my chest last night in the movie room and only made it back to her house a few hours ago.

Andie: so my dad left town this morning

Me: U okay?

Her reply comes within seconds, and I imagine that, like me, she's still in bed.

Andie: I'm fine.

Andie: But I'll be GREAT when u send me the next chapter of Out of the Feral Lands

Andie: bonus points if theres kissing

Laughing, I hop out of bed and tiptoe past Patrick asleep in his bunk. On the way from my bed to my desk, I catch a glimpse of myself in the mirror and almost don't recognize the guy who's grinning from ear to ear. After hitting Send on the email, I look out my window, squinting at the bright sun and blue skies. Andie's dad seems to have taken the storm with him. I shoot her another text.

Me: Sent!

Andie: I'm being serious about the kissing, Tommy. It better be good!

Me: ur kind of strict

Me: I kind of like it

Andie: Tommy (don't know ur middle name) Ling are u flirting with me?

I'm not sure how to answer that question. Or how I *should* answer it, to be exact.

I absolutely *was* flirting with her.

At this point, flirting with Andie Weaver just feels natural. If I'm honest, every time I'm with Andie—whether it's texting her, watching a movie with her, eating pizza with her, *not* jumping off a rock with her, or just baring my soul on a dock in the rain—it all feels natural. Especially after last night. Having Andie curled up next to me, cheek resting on my chest, felt . . . right. She couldn't have seen more than twenty minutes of that movie before she was completely knocked out.

"Who are you texting this early in the morning, man?"

Patrick's voice punches through my thoughts, and faster than I can stop him, he's swiping my phone out of my hands. Before I know it, he's halfway across the room, studying the phone screen.

"Not cool, man," I say, exasperated. But it doesn't even register with him.

Patrick's eyes dart up to mine. "*Were* you flirting with her?" he asks, with a bite to his voice. He tosses the phone back to me. It's a long throw, but I catch it easily.

After sliding the phone back onto the desk, and far out of his reach, I head over to my bunk. If I'm going to have *this* conversation with my brother, I'm gonna need to sit down. I've wanted to confront Patrick about what really happened on the beach last summer with Andie ever since I found out on the Fourth of July. But he's always with Bekah or the guys, and this needs to be a brother-to-brother conversation.

"I've got a better question," I say, figuring I'll just get right to the point. "What the hell was that you pulled on the beach with her last summer, and when are you gonna make it right?"

Patrick rests his elbows on his knees and clasps his fingers together, letting his head fall between his shoulders for a few seconds. When he looks back up at me, he releases a whoosh of air. "I know, man. I know," he says, before rubbing the back of his neck and then falling back onto the bed. "I really didn't mean to hurt her or embarrass her like that," he says, voice raw like he's genuinely sorry. "It was just this small, stupid thing that got out of hand."

"I don't think anything about playing with someone's feelings is small or stupid," I tell him. And then, maybe for more reasons than one, I ask, "Did you even like her? Or was it all a joke?"

Patrick sighs. "It wasn't a joke. I swear," he insists, sitting up and meeting my eyes. "I really thought there could be something with us. Evan said the kiss could test it and Maisy would be my Get Out of Jail Free card."

"Sounds real dumb when you say it out loud, doesn't it?" I ask him flatly, trying to keep calm despite being even angrier now on Andie's behalf.

His eyes dart up to mine. "How long has this thing between you two been going on?"

"What thing?" I ask, feeling defensive. "Me and Andie are friends."

"Friends who flirt?" he lobs back, one eyebrow raised.

"Pat, you have a girlfriend," I remind him, wondering how this got turned around on me so fast.

"Dude, that's not why I'm asking," he says. He raises both hands. "I wanna know if you're into her. For *you*. I'm trying to talk to my brother about his feelings."

"Oh," is all I manage to say. It's my turn to rub the back of my neck. Because, honestly, it's way too early for this.

Maybe I take too long to figure out a response, because

Patrick just shakes his head and stands to walk toward the door. Before he opens it, he turns back to me. "Look, bro, this has been a good talk," he says before dramatically placing a hand over his heart and adding, "Just try not to hurt her."

Then he smirks, and I chuck a pillow at him to knock that shit-eating grin right off his face. He closes the door before it makes contact.

I admit I'm relieved that he seems to be in good spirits after the conversation he walked in on last night in the kitchen with our parents. And deep down I know he cares about Andie—though he's done a shitty job of showing it.

Even if he was joking, at the rate things are going, I might be the one most likely to get hurt in all of this. I still don't know if I'm more than a replacement for Patrick just yet. But after last night, I do know that Andie sees me as more than just the emotional-support-gerbil-turned-pig she's been leaning on all summer.

After I put on the Drew Barrymore flick, I caught more than a few not-so-subtle vibes from her. I felt it in the way she couldn't seem to keep her eyes on the screen. And the way she practically melted into me when I stopped fighting the urge to touch her. It felt like fighting off a pack of gorillas trying to keep myself from knocking over the popcorn and dried mango and pulling her close so we could watch the movie with nothing, not even space, between us. Eventually I gave in, and we spent most of the night wrapped up in each other.

If she hadn't fallen asleep, I absolutely would have kissed her.

So, yes. Andie and I are friends who occasionally flirt and cuddle, and I don't know what any of it means, but as of this morning, I have no regrets. Now that I'm alone, I head back over to my desk to answer one of Andie's questions.

Me: My middle name is Kai Le

Me: after my grandfather

Andie: That's beautiful. What does it mean?

Me: according to my dad it means triumph and happiness

Andie: Thomas Kai Le Ling is gonna look 🔥 on a book one day

Me: from your lips to the stars Andie

CHAPTER TWENTY-THREE

"Last time we did this, I swore it would take hard drugs to get me out there again," Mel groans as we lace ourselves into our high-speed-death rentals.

Today the lake crew is gathered together for Augie's eighteenth birthday party at the Big Bear Ice Arena, and Mel is selflessly taking one for the team in the name of love. By sheer coincidence, Augie and Mel's dad share a birthday. So the parents have crashed the party, making this a free-for-all at the rink.

"You don't do drugs," I remind her while struggling to pull the skates over my thick fuzzy socks. "So, what's your excuse this time?"

"FOMO *is* a drug," she says plainly. "Plus, Augie promised he wouldn't let go."

"Aw, how sweet! Our very own Jack and Rose," I say, wobbling as I stand. I have to clutch the Plexiglas partition so I don't collapse and embarrass myself before I even hit the ice. "Except for the part where Rose *does* let go and Jack becomes one with the ocean."

"Hey! Spoiler alert!" Mel objects, tossing her flip-flop at me. "Augie and I only finished half the movie!"

"Hate to break it to you, but the *Titanic* is at the bottom of the ocean as we speak," I tell her. "It's hardly a spoiler that people lost their lives."

I can tell we're on the verge of debating fact versus fiction when Mel's dad, the co–birthday boy, skates up to the partition behind us. He's moving his hips to the beat of some throwback disco song that's currently blasting over the sound system.

"You two gonna talk all day, or are you gonna get out here on the ice?" he hollers over the music. He wiggles his eyebrows and pumps his fists while skating backward, moving his blades in a zigzag formation. It's all fun and games until he bumps into Mrs. Bridges, who was doing a fast two-foot spin. The collision takes them down. When they hit the ice, they cling to each other and bust out laughing.

"Aren't they just adorable?" I tease as we fumble our way toward the ice.

"Yeah, but I think they're gonna feel it tomorrow," Mel adds, barely hiding her embarrassment. "Hope they packed the Icy Hot."

Out on the ice, it's total chaos.

The playlist is a chaotic blend of nineties grunge and pop, early-2000s Top 40 hits, and random disco throwbacks. Augie's resorted to pushing Mel on a dolphin-shaped sled while she preens like it's *her* birthday. Mason and Olivia are vlogging their skate for her viral *What I Did This Summer* YouTube series. Mel's parents have recovered from their stumble and are now trying partner spins in the center of the ice. My mom and Mrs. Ling seem to be in a competition for who can get around the rink in the *most* amount of time possible—while Mr. Ling is on the sideline taking calls. Patrick and Bekah have formed a chain with Evan and Selina, taking fast laps around the rink.

And Tommy's nowhere in sight, making *me* the fifteenth wheel, who's currently struggling to stay upright. While clutching the cramp in my side, I skate over to the wall for support and dig into my pocket to shoot him a text: u MIA from this party by choice?

Below Tommy's messages sits an unread message from Patrick. The first five words read Andie I'm really sorry about . . . and I don't know the rest because I've been ignoring it for three days.

When Tommy doesn't respond immediately, I push off the wall in search of my own dolphin sled—all this work at *not* falling is starting to give me shin splints, too. But on my way off the ice, Patrick skates over, taking me by surprise—or hostage, given the fact that I couldn't speed off if I tried. I'm basically trapped.

"Hey, Andie, you having fun?" Patrick asks. He cuts his blades so now we're facing the same direction.

"Uhhh, yeah," I say, eyes darting around for Mel so I can send a *Help* signal. We haven't exchanged so much as a grunt since the Fourth of July party, let alone been chatty. Truth is, I'm still very hurt by his reveal. But most of all, I feel like he's just not the guy or friend I thought he was. "Just trying not to pull a hamstring."

He laughs even though I wasn't kidding. Then his expression falls into a series of hard lines. "Andie, I just need you to know that I'll be sorry forever for how I made you feel on the beach last summer," he says. "I was lucky to be your friend and a fool to mess it up."

Whoa. As far as apologies go, that's a pretty good one. No excuses. No sharing blame. Just pure accountability. I'm standing, barely upright, processing what he's just said, when he takes the opportunity to fill the awkward silence.

"And since it looks like you and Tommy are hanging out these days . . ." At this point, my heart stutters. I almost trip and have to grab ahold of his sweatshirt to keep from falling. "I guess I just wanted you to know that I fully support it if you decide to—"

"Okay! Patrick, appreciate the apology, but we're *not* going there," I cut him off. "Plus, isn't he supposed to be getting back together with Chloe?"

I'm fishing for intel before I can stop myself. I can't lie—I'm hoping for a swift, decisive denial. Instead he looks thoughtful for a moment and opens his mouth to speak, but then Augie skates up to us pushing Mel on the sled.

"Is this guy bothering you, queen?" she asks, crossing her arms and giving him the stank face. Ever since Mel found out about Patrick and Evan's little stunt, she's been giving them the cold shoulder too.

I'm about to tell her we're fine when a crash and scream from across the rink cuts into our conversation.

"Heyyyyy, Bekah," I say while slowly approaching the bench where she's got her leg propped up on ice. My skates are off, so moving around is much easier. I take a seat, looking down with a grimace at her pineapple-size foot. "I'm really sorry about your ankle."

"Thanks, Andie," she says with a shrug. "I'm sorry everyone got to witness how much of a klutz I am."

We both laugh, and it's the first glimpse of a normal interaction I've had with her all summer.

"Well, look at it this way," I say. "Now you and Patrick can have a fun story for your kids one day."

And just like that, the normal is out the window. I could smack myself for saying the words as soon as they leave my mouth. I was aiming for lighthearted—funny, even. But instead I took a hard left and hit the bull's-eye for over-the-top. Cringing at myself, I rush to fix it. "I didn't mean to imply that you two are getting married and having babies anytime soon—*if ever.* But it's totally cool if you do choose to do that. I mean, if it's what you want." Bekah's staring at me now like she's concerned I may be experiencing a mild stroke. "You know what? I'll stop talking now. I just want you to know I'm rooting for you two."

Finally I shut up, as promised, and take a long, slow sip of my slushie. A few seconds of awkward silence pass between us, and the song switches over to Paramore's "Ain't It Fun."

"Thank you," she says, smiling and generously sidestepping my verbal diarrhea. "I'll be real—I didn't know if you were into him at the start of the summer. So it means a lot for you to say that."

My face heats up, and I feel sweat at my temples. Even so, her honesty feels kind of refreshing. I could get used to *not* walking on eggshells by pretending there hasn't been an elephant in the room every time the three of us are in the same place. Because of this, I decide to be honest too.

"When I came to the lake, *before* I knew you existed, I

was still into Patrick," I admit. "But I know we were never really right for each other in that way. Especially now that I see him with you. You guys look happy, and I'm happy that he's happy."

"Look at us," she says with a wink. "Being all mature and demure."

"Love that for us," I say back, and we lean in, tapping our shoulders together, before turning back to the ice.

With August almost here, time has been running out for our group to attempt the annual "all-nighter." It's the night we pick to sneak out and camp either on a boat or on the beach. Chances are that if we told our parents, they would agree to let us have our fun, with some restrictions. But where's the adventure in that?

This all started the summer after freshman year, when Augie's parents took a last-minute business trip to Palm Desert, giving us the chance to "borrow" their pontoon boat for the night. Shockingly, we pulled it off, and now we're on to our third annual attempt. Our strategy involves meticulous coordination via group chat and waiting up until all our parents have gone to bed. And because the Lings' primary suite is practically soundproof, Patrick and Tommy's house is usually the designated rallying point. If all goes to plan, by midnight Patrick will send the bat signal for us to meet up at the dock with coolers full of snacks, booze, tents, and sleeping bags. From there we pile into the boat and motor across the lake to our camping spot. As long as no one ends up arrested or hospitalized, our parents are totally clueless. We picked tonight, and Mel's dock this time, since her parents are gone for a wedding in Lake Arrowhead and won't be back until tomorrow evening.

In years past, Tommy's always been absent from the all-nighter, making one excuse or another. But this year he's coming, thanks to me. And all it took was a little convincing.

Tommy: sry I missed the skate party

Tommy: my dad set up another zoom with that scout

Andie: omg how did it go???

Tommy: fine, just "exploratory" blah blah

Andie: sounds like a party

Tommy: 🎉

Andie: speaking of . . . PLEASE tell me ur coming to the all-nighter tonight

Tommy: what do I get if I do?

Andie: . . . hmmm

Andie: I'll let you read my very first fic

Andie: it's SPICY

Tommy: sold

Andie: that was easy

Tommy: if only you knew

Andie: no Tommy, if only YOU knew

Andie: Oh and one more thing

Tommy: yes . . .

Andie: You have to rewrite the ending. I'll never forgive you if Sonam betrays Maxis by striking a deal with the Heir King for her freedom. Srsly this is crap, Tommy! Crap!

Tommy: issa tragedy . . . remember

Andie: only bc ur FORCING it to be!

Andie: Sonam and Maxis are m2b 4eva and u know it

Andie: just think about it ok?

Tommy: if u say so . . . but only bc u asked so nicely 😇

Selina's speaker battery died about half an hour ago, so tonight's camping soundtrack is a nature's chorus of crickets and bullfrogs. It's the middle of the night, and our sliver of a moon makes the sky so dark that countless stars peek through like tiny sparkling holes in a massive black blanket. Right now we're all huddled up in the boat and on our second game of the night since we had to give up Uno when the lamps we'd packed died on us too.

"All right, Tommy, truth or dare?" Mel shouts from across the pontoon, where she's sitting on Augie's lap.

"Dare," he answers casually. Like he didn't even consider the other option.

I turn over my shoulder and raise a questioning eyebrow at him. He winks at me and shrugs. Tommy's next to me with his arms outstretched, resting on the boat's railing. I've got a blanket draped over our legs where we're just an inch apart—something that I've been trying to ignore, but it's pretty much all I'm thinking about. It's funny to think that at the beginning of the summer we had to be forced to partner up for beer pong, and now we naturally find our way to each other.

"Oh-kaaay, Tommy-Boy," Augie says, mischievously rubbing his hands together. "I dare you to strip and jump in the lake."

"Are you kidding, Augie?" Mel shouts before swatting him on the arm. "What if, like, a leech latches onto his bare ass?"

Augie shrugs. "We've got salt," he casually reminds her while sporting a grin.

Mel shakes her head. "I can't watch," she moans, rolling her eyes and turning her head.

For my part, I have no words. Just hot cheeks and flaming interest in seeing Tommy Ling in his natural form. Of course, it would be better without an audience, but a girl will take what she can get.

Meanwhile, he's accepted his fate without complaint. He strips off his hoodie and tosses it to me. "Keep that warm for me. And close your eyes," he says, flashing those bright whites. I pull the hoodie on like I've been instructed, and get a whiff of Tommy's delicious scent as I do.

This exchange draws hoots and squeals from the group, who no doubt have already started to question what's going on between us. But I'm too focused to care. Because when Tommy stretches his arms over his head, I'm distracted by his bronze abs, letting my eyes linger for a few seconds. When he starts undoing his belt buckle, I at least have the decency to tuck my head into my hands.

"All right, ladies, nothing to see here," Patrick announces from the other side of the boat before he reaches up to cup his hands over Bekah's eyes.

Selina chimes in with, "You mean nothing we haven't already seen before." She laughs as Evan's hands go up to shield her eyes too.

"Hopefully, some things have changed since we all went streaking on the beach a few summers ago," Tommy says, just before we hear the telltale splash of him hitting the water.

Once he's in, we all open our eyes and cheer.

"Tommy, you really oughta work on your tan, bro! Your ass just blinded me!" Mason shouts from the bow of the boat.

"Shut up and throw me my shorts, man!" Tommy shouts, wiping the strands of wet hair from his eyes

He's swimming toward the shore with a huge smile on his face, and I can't look away. In the years that Tommy skipped out on these all-nighters, I thought maybe we weren't cool enough for him. But these past few weeks, he's made more than a joke of all my assumptions. Now I simply see him as someone I should have tried harder to get to know all along.

"Careful," Mel whispers into my ear. "Those heart-eyes are screaming, girl."

I nudge her in the ribs with my elbow, and we laugh. Then, suddenly, we're not laughing, because Tommy has fully emerged from the water, both hands covering the NSFW parts, but everything else is on full display. Mason thought it would be funny to toss his clothes several feet away from the shore. So now he has to tiptoe around the beach to find them, providing me a full view of every smooth, muscled inch of him. It should be illegal to look that good after jumping into cold, leech-filled water.

"Don't mind me," Tommy shouts. "Just freezing my ass off over here."

"I think that's your cue," Mel whispers into my ear. She's right. I've been sitting frozen admiring the view, but now I spring into action.

It takes me a minute to climb out of the boat, pick up his clothes, and walk over to him, all with my hand shielding him from view. I hold his shorts out in his general direction, and when he takes them from me, I feel a brush of his hand, warm despite the chill.

There's rustling, and then it quiets. "You can open your eyes now," he says, voice low. "I'm decent."

I drop my hand and try to keep my face as sweet and innocent as possible. "Who says I ever closed them?"

"Okay, who's next? Truth or dare?" Mel asks.

"I'll go," says Olivia. "Truth."

We all turn to Tommy, who's back in the boat and drying himself off with a towel. "Okay, Olivia, tell us what you're most afraid of."

Everyone says, "Oooooohhhh." Olivia takes a second to think, looking up at the starry sky. "That this, right now, is as good as things will ever get," she says. "That five, maybe ten years down the line, I'll look back at high school and say, *Wow, I really peaked.*"

"Damn!" Mel shouts. "That's de-pressing!"

"Okay, yes," Mason chimes in. "But my girl's honest, right? I mean, my dad's always talking about how high school is when he made some of the best and worst decisions of his life."

"Right," Augie says, looking really skeptical. "That's just propaganda our folks tell us to trick us into not doing stuff that gets us arrested."

We all laugh until Mel pushes the game along. "Okay, who's next?"

"I'll go," I say before I take a swig of my hard cider—likely the only drink I'll be having tonight. Tommy's fully dressed and settled back next to me, and I can feel his eyes boring into my profile. I'm still wearing his hoodie, which I have no intention of returning anytime soon.

"All right, Andie," she says with a sly smirk on her face. "What'll it be, truth or dare?"

I take a deep breath. In and out. "Dare."

Blame it on the alcohol. All 5 percent of it in this can. But Tommy's *truth* question got me in my feelings, and I feel like *doing* something to get me out of them. I'd rather kiss Mel on the lips or moon all of them than spill my guts tonight anyway.

"I dare you to kiss Tommy," Olivia says, and either my hearing temporarily cuts out or there's complete silence in the boat for the next five seconds.

My eyes dart over to Tommy, who's suddenly admiring the floor of the boat. His damp hair hides his eyes. In this moment I have absolutely no idea what to do. I want to kiss Tommy. Have wanted to since he pulled me close against his chest on that checkered dance floor. But when I think about all the eyes on this boat, a pit forms in my stomach, and suddenly I'm flashing back to last summer on the beach. A kiss I'd built up in my mind for years that crashed and burned in front of an audience. When I kiss Tommy Ling, I don't want company.

"What are the rules if you skip out on a dare?" Patrick asks, taking me by surprise. I didn't expect him to be so locked in to my decision.

"Uh, she has to take a shot," Mel says, somberly lifting a handle of tequila. She knows how much I hate that stuff.

Now everyone's staring and waiting—like it's Final Jeopardy and I scammed my way into this last round. And it's this exact feeling, like I'm under a microscope, that brings up bitter memories of last summer. PTSD is real, and right now I feel frozen.

I look at Tommy, wishing on every star that I could read his face right now. If I follow my gut and opt out, will he be offended or relieved? Have I misread the signals sparking between us the last few weeks? Or does he want to kiss me but doesn't want it to be a spectacle either? Not to mention the Chloe of it all. Since the Fourth, we've only gotten closer, and he hasn't mentioned any more texts from her. But for all I know, they could either be back to no contact or planning a full-out reconciliation—something that would, no doubt, send me to the bottom of a box of wine or a tub of rocky road.

"What's it gonna be, sugar lips?" Mason prods, and Selina playfully smacks him on the back of the head.

I hesitate for another second, just in case Tommy decides to give me a sign. But his expression is totally unreadable. For the first time all summer, I feel like he's hung me out to dry. I clear my throat. "I'll, um . . . I'll take the shot."

The second I say the words, Tommy releases a deep sigh—like he's been holding his breath. Next, Mel's passing me the shot of that diabolical tequila and I feel like I deserve the harsh burning sensation I get as it courses down my throat.

Truth or dare ended with Patrick climbing a tree, Augie admitting that the most embarrassing place he's sprung an erection was at a teeth cleaning, and Mel having to sing the theme song from *Titanic* in its entirety. While all of this went down, Tommy and I didn't speak. But we didn't move away from each other, either. Just sat under the warm blanket as the awkward tension mounted between us.

Now it's three a.m. and Augie's snoring. Patrick and Bekah are cuddled together near the helm of the boat. I'm watching them now, and this time, the dull ache that bloomed in my chest when I saw them all snuggled up at the Summer Kickoff party is nowhere to be found. I feel absolutely nothing. Maybe this is what moving on feels like.

A few inches to my right where Tommy's sleeping is a different story. He nodded off about fifteen minutes ago, which means I've had fifteen minutes to study the dark fan of his eyelashes lying across the tops of his cheeks, the long slope of his nose, and the scruff peppered across his upper lip and cheeks. I'm so busy studying his features, working my way down to his neck, that when I take a brief detour back up to his face, I'm shocked to find that he's been watching me. Eyes open and fully awake.

"Sneaky," I whisper, smiling.

"Creepy," he says back with a smirk.

Playfully I swat at him. He catches my hand, brings it to his mouth, and kisses the inside of my palm. And I can't help the sound that comes out of my mouth. Next he's curling his fingers around the back of my neck and bringing his forehead to mine. I grab ahold of his wrist. Our eyes latch for one second before they fall shut, a question and an answer without words. Then he presses his mouth to mine.

And now I'm kissing Tommy Ling on the back of a pontoon boat, and it's nothing like my first kiss with Everett Walker. That kiss felt like scribbling outside the lines. But this—this kiss is a masterpiece. It's soft and slow and sweet and warm.

It's *Tommy*.

He shifts his weight, angling us so that he's slightly on top of me. Just when the kiss really deepens, Tommy pulls away. I want to protest, but I also don't want us to get carried away. After all, we're not alone on this boat.

He settles back in beside me, and our lips meet again, with less urgency now. We kiss for so long, the sky turns a shade of blue gray. With one final tug on my bottom lip, Tommy gently pulls away. "We should get some sleep," he suggests, his voice raspy and raw.

My immediate yawn is proof that he's right. I nod, and he tucks me into him, my back to his chest. I know he's out for good when his breathing slows against my back. I'm about to fall under myself when my phone buzzes in my front pocket. Thinking it could be a text from my mom, I reach into my front pocket to check it, and that's when I remember that I'm wearing Tommy's hoodie. Because this is not my phone. And the text isn't from my mom.

It's four a.m., and here I am, sandwiched between Tommy Ling and a message from his ex-girlfriend.

Chloe: Can I see you Friday?

I kissed Andie Weaver.

Who knew all-nighters came with so many surprises? If I had known, maybe I wouldn't have skipped them before. I could have kissed Andie until the sun came up if only just to make up for all the times I've wanted to all summer but held myself back.

But every surprise wasn't great.

When I got my hoodie back from Andie, I found another text from Chloe. When I responded to her *I miss you* text on the Fourth, she sent a string of messages about how she'd made a mistake and wanted us to get back together. She told me she'd be visiting the mountains with her parents in a few weeks and asked if we could meet up. I told her I'd be around and to just reach out. Now she wants to meet up tomorrow to "clear the air."

After the night I just had with Andie Weaver, I've got all the clarity I need.

According to the group chat, everyone made it back to our respective houses before their parental units woke up. After waking up, Andie barely said two words to me before running off with Mel after we docked. I tried not to over-think it because Augie's alarm didn't go off on time, and we were all stressed about not getting busted. I was so exhausted from the rush of kissing her coupled with the awkward sleeping arrangements that I totally crashed when I got home.

It's almost noon when I finally peel my eyes open in the bunk room. I'm not surprised to see that Patrick's gone and the room's brightly lit up by the sun. But I *am* surprised to find my dad sitting at my desk with my open laptop in front of him.

I shoot up out of bed and struggle to find my voice. "Dad, what are you doing?" I ask, and it comes out scratchy and hollow.

He startles and turns. Almost instantly his face resets with a serious hard line. "Tommy, I owe you an apology," he says, and I'm close to pinching myself to make sure this isn't a dream. "For the other night, and for a long time before that."

"Uh, thanks?" is all I can manage. We haven't spoken much since our talk in the kitchen, just moved around each other in a cloud of polite tension.

He turns toward my laptop and points at the screen. "Why didn't you ever show your mom and me your writing?"

"You never asked," I say, surprised at the direction this is going.

"Fair." He scratches the scruff on his chin. "You know, I didn't realize you and Andie had gotten so close this summer," he says. I have no idea where he's going with this, but I am very curious. "She told me she'd been reading your book when we were in line for skates at Augie's party. Said I should give it a try. Tommy . . . what I just read . . . well, it's *really* good. I mean, I'm no expert or anything. You know I read about sports and business and things like that. But I had no idea you had a whole world of characters going on up there." He gestures to his head.

Yesterday, if you'd asked me if I needed my dad to compliment my writing, I'd have easily said no. But what he's just said feels better than pitching a dozen no-hitters. And if I already couldn't get Andie off my mind after we finally kissed, finding out that she talks me up when I'm not even around seals the deal. I'm falling for this girl.

"That's what you've been doing all this time, huh?" Dad asks, a small smile creeping across his face.

"Yeah," I say, smiling back and nodding. We've never

had a moment like this, and I wish I could bottle it.

"That's what you want to do at school?" he asks. "You want to write these fantastic sci-fi worlds and stuff like that?"

I nod again.

He seems to consider this for a minute. "I came in here to tell you that I should have handled our conversation the other night in the kitchen a lot better," he says. "And that's *not* just because your mother told me to say this.

"You, your mom, and Patrick . . . you're everything to me," he says, and I'm surprised to hear his voice crack. Looking closer, I notice that his eyes are shining. "I want you to be stand-up young men who follow through on your commitments. But more than that, I want you to be happy with your decisions. I don't want you to have regrets because you got pushed in a direction that I made you choose. You following me?"

"Yeah, Dad. I get what you're saying," I tell him, still taking it all in.

"Well, I was thinking maybe you redshirt this year," he suggests. "Then you could keep your athletic scholarship at UC but take the pressure off and explore other interests."

That sounds like all I ever wanted. "What about the scout?" I ask.

"I talked to him," Dad says. "He appreciated you meeting with him. Says he'll be around when you're rea *if* you're ready to talk about trying out in a year."

We sit for a beat just taking each other in. Honestly, I don't really know what to say. I wonder if things could have gone smoother if I'd talked to my dad about this a year ago. But I couldn't have asked for a better result than where we are now.

"So," I say, pointing at the laptop, "you think I'm best-seller material?"

"You're a Ling, and that's good enough for me," Dad says, and his pat on the back turns into a quick hug before we head up to the kitchen for what smells like pancakes and bacon.

And after scarfing down a breakfast of champions, I head back downstairs to rewrite the ending for Sonam and Maxis. It's one I can almost guarantee will be Andie-approved.

> The Heir King stood before his throne, wrapped in golden threads from head to toe. These were not his garments for battle. They were his robes for judgment. Flanked by armed guardsmen, he stood as an impenetrable force—prepared to sentence Sonam and Maxis.
>
> When the king spoke, his voice sent echoes across the chamber, and all fell silent.
>
> "Sonam Aurelia and Maxis Oshe, your sentence is banishment from the Feral Lands. You

will live out your lives as Time Exiles. For defying the king's decree, you will cease to exist in the modern era. Even the memory of you will be wiped clean from the consciousnesses of those who knew you. At sunrise, you are to report to the Eye to take the leap of fate, where you will travel to a new age to serve your sentence in the next lifetime."

And when he finished speaking, the guardsmen apprehended the prisoners as the crowd broke into chaos, for Sonam and Maxis would be the first of the Usher class to be banished.

"Sonam!" Maxis called out, but she couldn't hear him over her cries. The guards pulled the lovers in opposite directions.

I love you—she mouthed the words. *I'm sorry.*

*****

Sonam stood at the edge of the Eye, a massive and dark oval-shaped hole at the center of the great temple of Oracles. From its center shone millions of tiny flickering stars, speckled across a sheet of the blackest black. Sonam found a shred of comfort by imagining that taking this leap of fate would be like jumping at the sky.

The guardsmen brought in Maxis. With his bloodstained clothes, swollen face, and faltering gait, she knew he'd been battered through the night by the king's henchmen. Sonam wanted to cry for him, but she'd not been fed nor given water, so she had no tears left. Her voice, too, had gone.

Again, she mouthed, *I love you, I'm sorry*—over and over as she watched Maxis approach the other side of the Eye.

When the guardsmen threw him to the ground, the Oracle stepped forward.

"Leave us," she commanded. The Oracle performed the blessing of the banished, and then there was nothing left but to take the leap.

"Jump first, Sonam," Maxis cried. "And I will find you in the next lifetime."

And so, she did. With closed eyes, her heart broken, but still somehow full of hope, Sonam jumped.

But Maxis was not far behind her.

Part I—The End

CHAPTER TWENTY-SIX

I kissed Tommy Ling.

I *kissed* Tommy Ling.

Or he kissed me? Either way, last night on a pontoon boat under a million stars and a crescent moon, our mouth anatomy connected, and I might never be the same. I could write a dozen *Vampire Diaries* fanfics and still never find the words to capture the feeling of thinking I had potential with Patrick, only to discover that the real connection is with *his brother*.

But this morning, when I wake up to the sound of my mom's Latin Zumba class on YouTube, the panic swoops in like a flash flood to overshadow my ecstasy. Because what was that text from Chloe? Has he responded to her? Is he seeing her Friday? As in *tomorrow.*

On the Fourth of July, Tommy admitted to me that he missed her. And who could blame him? They were together for practically a year and she broke things off abruptly, and for silly reasons, if you ask me. If you want the guy to get out of his head, all you gotta do is offer him a penny for his thoughts, and he'll sing like a bird! Clearly Chloe wasn't trying very hard.

Blame it on the moonlight, the alcohol, or the impending summer's end, but last night felt like the start of something between us. But what if he's not over his ex?

I realize I could be overthinking things, just like I did with Patrick. We kissed. We flopped. I panicked, froze, and ghosted him for a month, then spent a year blaming it all on myself when it turns out it wasn't even real to begin with. And who wants to go down *that* path again?

I'm about to put on my "Crashing Out" playlist when Mom calls from downstairs. "Andie! Mel's here!"

It takes a beat for me to realize what time it is. But when I do, I dart out of bed and throw my hair into a topknot. I totally forgot that I promised to help with the photo project Mel's planning to submit as part of her portfolio application to SCAD—it's got something to do with capturing the "fleeting essence" of summer and youth and nature and all that.

"Be down in a minute!" I holler down the hall.

Scrambling, I run to my bathroom to brush my teeth and change into my bathing suit and cover-up. Then I head over to my dresser to grab some sunscreen, sandals, and my tote. At the last minute, I double back for my phone.

After taking the steps two at a time, I almost trip at the bottom when I find not just Mel but Augie *and* Tommy standing in the foyer.

At first, he's laughing at something with Augie, but at the sound of my footsteps, Tommy turns to me, and a slow smile spreads across his face. Despite what I saw on his phone, I can't help but smile back. He looks *good*. Tall and tan in a green polo that matches his eyes.

I want to kiss him again. But we've had zero time to talk about last night and what it means for us and the rest of the summer. And now I can sense the growing panic rising again inside me. Like climbing the rock face at Azure Falls and preparing to jump. I want this, but I am *so* afraid.

I must look like a deer in headlights, because Mel rushes to explain what they're doing here. "I needed extra models," she says. "Tommy volunteered, and Augie didn't have a choice."

Last night, or this morning to be exact, Mel's phone died, and Augie accidentally set his alarm for p.m. instead of a.m. So we all overslept and missed our sunrise deadline to sneak back home. Still, we made it by the skin of our teeth. Everyone confirmed via group text that they got back inside before any of our parents found out we'd gone missing. Which means we've got another successful all-nighter in the books. It also means that I didn't get a chance to tell Mel about the Kiss. Even still, I think I want to keep what happened with me and Tommy last night between us for now.

Mom sends us off with a full picnic spread, and I'm the last one out the door. Before I close it behind me, she lightly tugs at my wrist. "Hey, Andie-Bug," she says, her eyes searching my face. "When you get back, can we have a chat?"

For a second, I assume I've been busted—like maybe she caught me sneaking back inside on the Ring camera.

"It's nothing bad, I promise," she says, dispelling my worries. "Just something I've been meaning to talk to you about since your dad's visit."

I'm relieved I won't be grounded, but now I'm anxious for new reasons. Since Dad's visit last week, Mom and I haven't touched the topic of his engagement and how I already knew about it with a ten-foot pole. However, the other day, Dad called to invite me over for dinner with Trishell, his now fiancée, when I get back to Los Angeles. I haven't told Mom about this part yet, and the whole thing just gives me a queasy feeling, to be honest.

"Sure," I say with a smile. "I'll text when we're headed back."

She playfully tugs on a loose strand of my hair before I turn to join the others, who've packed into Augie's Jeep.

With Augie driving and Mel riding shotgun, my only option is to slide into the back with my brand-new late-night make-out buddy. Luckily, Augie's got his cab fully open, because the tension between me and Tommy might otherwise cause spontaneous combustion.

When I shut the door and Augie peels out, I can feel the heavy weight of Tommy's gaze on the right side of my face. After putting up hard resistance for all of sixty seconds, like a magnet, I can't help but turn to him.

"So, you want to talk about last night?" he asks quietly after a long stretch of the waiting game.

I peek up front and see that Mel and Augie are busy bickering loudly over the lyrics to "One Week" by Barenaked Ladies.

"We could," I say, trying to keep my voice low while my heart's racing. I wonder if he can tell. "But the first rule of all-nighters is, we don't talk about what happens at the all-nighters." I mean it as a joke. My way of keeping things light, in case he's about to tell me about Chloe's text and that they've got plans for a date soon—you know, emotional-support-pig duties and all.

"Oh-kay," he says, eyebrows furrowing. "Well, I just think it would be good for us to . . . you know. Get on the same page about . . . us?" He whispers the last word, and I'm thankful. I trust Mel with my secrets, but Augie is a blabbermouth.

"Oh, right," I say, tucking my hair behind my ears, then

fiddling with my purse strap. I'm finding it hard to look him in the eye. "Okay, well, you go first." I can feel the heat rise in my cheeks when I make the suggestion.

He takes a deep breath, and that's when I do look over at him. When our eyes meet, my stomach does a backflip. Holy crap, this boy is beautiful. Next, he's stretching his hand across the center seat, reaching for me. Then we're holding hands, fingers locked—Augie and Mel can get an eyeful, for all I care.

I watch our hands for long seconds as his thumb gently traces circles on the back of my palm. I don't want to say anything that might break the spell between us. He said he wanted us to get on the same page. Well, this *feels* like we are. I'm about to tell him just that, when the car takes a sudden swerve and Mel screams.

"I'd rather die than smell like this for another second," Mel moans as she hangs her head out the passenger-side window of the Jeep.

I'm in the back, pouring a bottle of water over my face, but even that seems to have sustained a hit, because it smells like ass too.

"Come on, babe. It's not that bad," Augie says through a choke and a cough as he pulls off the main road toward the swimming hole at Azure Falls, the main stop on Mel's shot list. "I've smelled worse in a locker room."

"You've smelled worse than the fully expressed anal glands of a skunk?" Tommy asks in disbelief. And I don't think I've ever seen a human turn his current shade of green.

"Well, when you put it that way," Augie says, "probably not."

Augie made a violent swerve to avoid a little black-and-white critter that was crossing the road. Lucky for the skunk, Augie's response time was fast enough to spare its life. But it still got spooked enough to spray us with a noxious cloud of funk. Augie throws the car into park, and we all bust out of our seat belts and barrel toward the swimming hole, stripping down to our bathing suits as we go.

Mel sets her camera on a rock, and we all dive into the glistening pool. Odds are, it's going to take a lot of time and even more soap to fully rid us of the stench. But at least the swimming hole can take the edge off long enough for the Jeep to air out before we head back into town.

The four of us tread water in silence, likely all trying to block out what just happened.

After a minute or two, I give voice to what I assume we've all been thinking. "At least he survived," I say. "Otherwise, we'd be holding a makeshift funeral on the side of the road right now."

Mel grimaces. "Don't judge me, but that could have made for some awesome photos."

"Yep," Augie says. "I'm *definitely* judging you on that one, babe."

Mel splashes him in the face, which starts a playful water fight between the lovebirds and leaves me and Tommy alone treading water.

"Are you thinking what I'm thinking?" I ask as a smile creeps across my lips.

He wiggles his eyebrows suggestively. "Depends on what you're thinking."

Laughing, I splash him with water, then point up to the diving ledge. "For old times' sake?"

He raises his eyebrows. "You sure?"

I shrug and say, "What do I have to lose?"

We're three-quarters of the way up and haven't stopped once. Maybe our brush with death on the road did something to shock the fear of heights out of me. Or maybe it's the feeling of limitlessness that comes from liking a boy who likes you back. Or it could be the funk still clinging to us like a helpful distraction. Either way, I'm impressed with myself.

"We almost made it, thank God!" Mel shouts, huffing and puffing with her hands braced on her hips. "Whose idea was this again?"

"Andie's!" Tommy and Augie remind her in unison. Tommy's bringing up the rear, with Augie taking the lead.

When we finally make it to the top, Mel and Augie are up first for their jump. It all feels strangely familiar. Except this time, I'm not seeing double and my stomach hasn't threatened to escape through my throat . . . yet.

"Remember to shoot for the center of the water," Tommy shouts. And it's a good thing he does, because, let's face it, we can't afford another mishap today.

Mel turns back and throws him two thumbs-ups. "Aye, aye, Captain!" she shouts, before giving Augie a big kiss on the cheek. A few seconds later, they are airborne and I'm ignoring the small ominous flutter in my stomach.

We hear their shouts of joy on the way down, and then a big splash signals their safe entry. I breathe a sigh of relief but keep my eyes screwed shut. I start whispering to myself, "I'm not a coward. I'm not a coward. I'm not a—"

I feel Tommy place his hands on my shoulders. Warm and slightly rough with calluses, they immediately calm me down. "Andie, you've got this," he says, piercing through my panic.

When I open my eyes, his face is just a few inches from mine. "What if I wimp out like last time?" I ask, my voice shaky and hollow.

"Well, how about this?" he says, smoothing his hands up to either side of my neck and interlocking his fingers at the back of my head. I step into him, and I'm hyperaware of all the places our bodies touch—the press of his stomach against mine, the light brush of our thighs. "You jump first, and I'll go right behind you? That way we guarantee you don't miss out this time."

I roll the idea around in my head for a few seconds. "Okay. Okay, I can do it," I say, more to myself than to him.

He smiles and leans in. I think he's going to kiss my lips, but he goes for my forehead instead. "You've got this," he says.

I walk up to the ledge and spend a few seconds visualizing myself falling from the mountain. I can see the moment I hit the water. And then it's an instant *nope* for me. I take several steps backward and turn to Tommy.

Like I'm on autopilot, I reach for his hand. "Jump with me, Tommy? Please?" I ask, embarrassed to sound like I'm begging.

Without hesitation, he takes my hand and joins me on the ledge. "On the count of three, we jump. Together," he says, and I nod before he counts us off.

"One,

two,

three."

Then we're in the air, falling, and falling some more. But never once letting go.

CHAPTER TWENTY-SEVEN

TOMMY

Below the surface, we've finally released our clasped hands. I open my eyes underwater, and a flash of green floating to the top sets me at ease. I come up for air, and Andie's face is the first thing I see—a smile so full and bright that I feel lucky she's aiming it at me. I might not know exactly how she feels about me, but in this moment, I can't pretend I don't know how *I* feel about her. I feel everything.

"We did it!" she says breathlessly, her eyes sparking with complete satisfaction. "Can you believe it?"

Laughing, I reach up to smooth back the wet hair from my eyes. "We did," I tell her.

She looks so proud, and despite the uncertainty about where we stand, I reach out to pull her into my chest and kiss her hair. I still haven't kissed her again the way we kissed last night. Call me old-school, but I feel like we should have a real conversation with actual words before we do that again. I feel ready to try with Andie. But we've still got so many unknowns. I'm heading to college in the fall. She's still got senior year to finish. All that we can figure out as it comes. The real issue is Chloe. It doesn't seem right to start something new with Andie without officially cutting that off first.

Andie and I freestyle our way over to the rock bed to find our towels. After whooping and cheering for Andie for finally making the jump, Mel took Augie off somewhere to snap photos. Either the persistent skunk stench has dulled my senses or our hour-long swim has done its job, because the smell seems to be fading by now. We're toweling ourselves off, but when I get down to my legs, I notice that something's wrong.

"Oh my God, Tommy! What did you do?" Instantly Andie's kneeling at my feet.

I sit on the ground to get a better look at the cut. Andie gently cradles my ankle with her hands, and while I'm embarrassed that she's so close to my huge foot, she seems determined to examine the open wound. A cut near my heel leaks a steady trickle of my blood onto the rocks. It isn't deep enough for stitches, but I'll need to get it cleaned up and bandaged fast to avoid infection.

Mel and Augie are out of sight now, probably hiking up the trail with her camera. With the two of us alone, Andie runs back to the Jeep for the first aid kit and gets back in under five minutes.

As she's tending to my wound, her fingers moving quickly and gently, neither of us says much. She just carefully works to clean the dirt and debris away before spraying the area with antiseptic and bandaging my heel with gauze and medical tape. Even though I don't love the circumstances, I do like feeling her touch and attention.

"How'd you get so good at this?" I ask, finally breaking the silence.

She smiles and pats my calf to signal that she's done. I reluctantly lift my foot from her lap, and we adjust our sitting positions so we're both looking out at the water.

"I coach youth soccer every fall and spring," she says. "Let's say I'm well versed in nursing cuts and bruises."

"Ah," I say. "The more you know."

"What more would you like to know about me, Tommy Ling?" she asks, leaning over and bumping me with her shoulder.

I'm about to ask her something completely unhinged like *Will you be my emotional support girlfriend?* when my phone starts to buzz on the towel between us. We both look down to stare at the five letters that are flashing on the screen: *Chloe*.

I look up and lock eyes with Andie. Because I already know who I want to be talking to right now. I'm sitting with her, smelling like skunk juice.

But her expression is unreadable. Probably the same as mine the night of truth or dare. I know she was looking to me for what to do, but I wanted her to make the choice on her own—to be fully in control of the moment. Especially after she very much wasn't last year with Patrick. Funny how the tables turn.

The call is on its fourth ring when she finally speaks. "I think you should answer that," Andie says flatly.

Chloe goes to voicemail as I sit watching Andie for a while longer. I'm trying to get a read on her, but I can't.

Maybe I was wrong about us. Maybe last night's kiss wasn't the *everything* to her that it was to me.

Then Chloe's calling again, and this time Andie breaks our eye contact. I can see Mel and Augie walking back through the clearing, and Andie gets up to join them.

Sighing, I answer the phone as she walks away. "Hey, Chloe."

"Tommy?" Chloe's voice is soft and sweet, just like I remember. "I thought you weren't going to pick up," she says. "I was about to leave a message."

"Sorry," I tell her. "Uhhh . . . what's up?"

"I didn't hear back from you after the Fourth," she says.

"So I get that you're busy, probably working on your book and stuff. But my parents have this thing in Arrowhead tomorrow. I can probably get away for an hour or so," she says. "I was thinking we could meet up and talk?"

I look across the rocks to where Andie's sitting with Mel now. They're both laughing, heads thrown back, not a care in the world. If we were on the same page about last night before, right now it feels like we're on different chapters.

"Tommy? Are you there?" Chloe asks.

"Uh, yeah. Sorry. I'm still here," I tell her, rubbing my temples because of the headache blooming there.

"Okay, well, as I was saying," Chloe goes on, "I think we owe it to each other to talk face-to-face."

I never responded to any of her messages about breaking up with me being a mistake. Honestly, I was overwhelmed and confused. But I'm not anymore. And I think she's right that she deserves to hear that from me in person.

"Um . . . . tomorrow's good," I say. "Just send me the address and I'll be there."

"Great!" she says, and I can hear the smile on her voice. "And, Tommy?"

"Yeah, Chloe?"

"I really do miss you."

The call drops before I can answer her. And it's probably the first time in my life that I'm grateful for bad reception.

CHAPTER TWENTY-EIGHT

"Well, what did you say when he told you he was going to meet her?" Mel's drink sloshes in her glass when she leans toward my lounge chair.

We're on her back porch trying to even out our tans while drinking Arnold Palmers, waiting for Mel's dad to finish up grilling on the lower deck. Her mom and mine are on the porch with us, pretending not to eavesdrop while they paint their toenails several feet away.

I slump down on my towel. "I told him how happy I am for them and I hope he drives safely."

Replaying the moment in my head feels just as painful as

it did in real time. It was just about sunset and past time for us to head back home. Mel had captured everything on her shot list, and frankly, we all needed hot showers.

Tommy and I sat in the back of the Jeep. This time, there was no hand-holding. Just two people with a whole lot of awkward tension and no place to release it. When I asked about his chat with Chloe and he said she wanted to meet up to talk at a diner in Lake Arrowhead, I swallowed down the sick feeling rising in my stomach and stuttered out something like *I hope you two can figure things out.* Then I rolled down my window and put in my earbuds. We didn't talk for the rest of the ride. When I got home, I ran upstairs and shut myself in my room, only opening the door when my stomach grumbled at the smell of the tomato bisque and grilled cheese that Mom had left in the hall for me. She likely knew I just wanted to eat my feelings when I'd texted asking if we could save our chat for another day.

"And what did your face look like when you said it?" Mel asks, deep in reporter mode. "I'm gonna need a visual before I can give you my expert opinion."

I mimic the forced smile that I gave Tommy. Mel frowns.

"Well, at this point, you only have yourself to blame," she says flatly before flopping over onto her stomach and closing her eyes.

"What was I supposed to say? *No, Tommy! Please don't go! Pick me, choose me, love me?*" I ask. "This isn't a TV show,

Mel. And if this summer proves anything, it's that *I'm* not the main character."

"Definitely not with that attitude!" Mel turns over to sit up in her lounge chair now. "Andie, I'm going to say this with love, so brace yourself." I don't think I've ever seen her this worked up before. "You know how we've always known Tommy as the quiet loner who does weird things like stuffing his laptop into ice coolers to protect it from the sun and jumping off rocks and stuff?"

"Yeah," I say, not knowing at all where this is going.

"Well, this summer we found out that Tommy Ling *can* open up. He just needs the right crowd. And apparently, that crowd is *you*. Also, he didn't *actually* stuff his laptop into that cooler on Ski Beach at the start of the summer. It was just an excuse he fed Mason and the guys because he'd packed a picnic *for you*," Mel says, pointing two bright orange nails at me.

I have no idea what she's talking about with the laptop-cooler thing. But I remember his picnic. My stomach does a flip and my chest flutters.

"And yeah, Tommy climbs rocks and jumps off them. But he's also patient enough to go at a grandma's pace and hold your hand so you can jump off too. The guy even sustained a flesh wound while doing it," she says. "You catching a common theme here?

"If not, let me make it clear," she says. "Did you ever consider the fact that maybe Tommy Ling agreed to be your emotional-support animal for the summer and ended up falling head over heels for you?"

Of course I considered that. Or maybe *fantasized* about it is the more accurate take. There *were* countless moments when I scared myself with how much I was enjoying our "arrangement" and hoping he was feeling the same. But then the doubt and fear would creep in. Was it all in my head like it had been with Patrick?

"Okay. Say you're right," I tell Mel. "How do we explain the fact that we kissed two nights ago and still he's on his way to meet up with his ex-girlfriend? I mean, all summer, he's seen how messed-up I am over Patrick and my parents. He's a smart guy. He writes romance-ish fiction! He has to know what this would do to me!"

"Okay! Let's scale back the drama, Audra McDonald." Mel's joke cuts into my verbal diarrhea. "Do you think maybe Tommy is the kind of guy who's fine risking his life jumping off cliffs but maybe a little hesitant to . . . I don't know, risk his heart with the girl who's spent the summer trying to move on from his brother?"

Her words hit me like a pie in the face, and I notice my mom looking at me too. Not saying a word. Just studying me from the comfort of her lounge chair.

Mel doesn't stop there. "I mean, I've been watching the two of you for weeks, and it would take a tranquilizer dart and heavy alcohol for me to miss the way he looks at you," she says, taking another sip of her drink. "And news flash, your eyes get all googly whenever he's around too. You've tried to hide it. But let's be for real for two seconds. It took years for you and Patrick to fumble a kiss and then stop being friends altogether. In a fraction of that time, you and Tommy had the best kiss of your life, and now you're both spiraling over each other."

"I wouldn't say he's spiraling," I tell her. "He went off after another girl."

"Andie. Sweet, sweet Andie," Mel says, patting my head. "This is my whole entire point. Tommy went after Chloe because you didn't give him a reason *not* to."

And there's the second pie to the face.

CHAPTER TWENTY-NINE

TOMMY

Chloe's sitting at a booth in the back corner of the diner. When I walk in, the chime over the door draws her attention, and when we lock eyes, she smiles and waves. A pit forms in my stomach.

I shouldn't have come.

"Eating alone?" The host greets me with a menu, and I tell her that I'm meeting someone before pointing toward Chloe's table. She leads me that way. I stuff my hands into my pockets and follow.

When I reach the booth, Chloe stands to pull me into a hug, and on instinct, my arms wrap around her waist. Her hair is long, straight, and brown like I remember. It even smells like I remember it. Cinnamon and vanilla. And she's wearing the yellow dress I always told her was my favorite. That only makes me feel even more guilty.

"I'm so happy you came," she says, her voice bright and sweet as I slide into the booth.

"I figured you were right—it's probably good for us to talk in person" are the first words I say. And it's true. I loved her for a year. She ended things over a text message. It seems only right that we get some closure face-to-face.

"So, Tommy," she starts, and with the way she's leaning in and batting her eyelashes, it's clear we aren't on the same page about this visit at all. "I've been thinking about the things I said at the start of the summer about us not being compatible, and I think it's something we can work on."

"Work on how?" I ask her, mainly because I want to understand her thinking.

"We just need to draw you out of your shell a little bit," she suggests with a small smile. "You're an introvert, I get it. You're not the best at making new friends. But that's what you have me for." She reaches across the table to place her hand on mine. I have the instinct to pull away, but I feel frozen, astonished by how I feel absolutely nothing at her touch.

"Actually, I *have* made some new friends this summer at the lake," I tell her.

"Oh?" she says, clearly surprised. She sits back against the booth. "Well, I want to meet them!"

"I've known them for a while," I explain, briefly looking out the window. "It's just that this summer's been kind of different. I started spending time with people I feel like I can really be myself around."

"That's great, Tommy." Chloe's face falls just slightly, like she's starting to catch on to what I'm really saying.

"One of them in particular," I add. "She even started reading the book I've been working on. You know, the one with the time-traveling exiles?"

Chloe just nods and starts to fiddle with the rim of her coffee mug. "What's her name?" she asks, her voice dropping low.

"Andie." I say her name and don't even realize I'm smiling until Chloe glances up at me.

"I see," she says. There's a finality to her words. She stares at me for a few beats, and then, without warning, she starts to pack up her purse and keys.

"Chloe?" I ask, leaning forward. "You don't have to run off. We can still catch up."

With a small smile and sad eyes, she settles back into the booth, even sets down her bag. "It's just . . . the way you said her name just now," she says, shaking her head just a little. "Andie. It's like you lit up when you thought about her. I've been wanting to feel that from you for a year. I wasn't lying when I said that I missed you."

"Chloe, I'm sorry. I—"

"You really don't need to apologize to me, Tommy," she says, raising a hand to stop me. "I shouldn't have broken things off the way I did with you. So *I'm* sorry. But whatever's going on with you and Andie seems really special. I hope you two can work it out."

With that, she slides out of the booth and stops to kiss me on the cheek before she walks away. And that's our official goodbye.

CHAPTER THIRTY

"I think it's time I tell you girls a story."

Mom takes a deep breath, settling in on her stool. We've come into the kitchen now that the mosquitoes have run us off the porch, though Mel's mom ran into town for more wine.

Over the course of the afternoon, our moms have gotten a speedy recap about my antics over the summer—how I accidentally fell for Tommy on a quest to get over his brother and how now Tommy's gone after his ex, *potentially* because he wants her back, but also potentially because I was too much of a chicken to tell him not to.

They sat and listened closely, my mom adjusting her thick-rimmed glasses at the juicy parts, like the Fourth of July slow dance and the truth-or-dare kiss. (We left out the part about sleeping on the boat.) And now, instead of addressing my crisis, she's giving us a history lesson.

"It was the year 2000. Honestly, this was a wild time in the world. We weren't supposed to make it that far, you know," she says, laughing. "It was Y2K. MTV was counting down to the end of the world."

Mel and I stare at each other in bewilderment. Mom laughs and says, "Girls, you'll just have to look it up."

She continues with her story. "Anyway, I was a junior in high school, and, Andie, you know your grandparents were stricter than the Santa Monica parking patrol. They would not let me date until I was old enough to drive. Dad's reasoning was that if I was ever out with a boy and got stranded or needed a way home, I'd be able to take care of myself. Looking back, it makes a lot of sense. But at sixteen, I thought it was oppression of the highest order."

Mom reaches up to tuck back a strand of hair that's fallen out of her messy bun. Mel and I are both leaning in, elbows on the counter, soaking up every ounce of the story. It's warm and glowy in the kitchen now, and we can feel the evening breeze drafting in from the open window.

"But back to my point. Junior year, I finally get my driver's license," Mom says, her eyes lighting up when she looks at me. "And, sweetie, Mama was a baddie—she had *options* when it came to the boys. But I was head over heels for just one of them—I mean, had it *bad*. Like Usher. We would sneak phone calls after my parents went to sleep. We would write letters. Sometimes he would even come up to the dance studio where I took ballet, after his baseball practices, so we could get just ten minutes alone to talk."

Mel and I share a quick glance. *Letters?*

"This boy knew that my parents ran a tight ship and that I wasn't allowed to date. But he was patient. He waited until I got my license. And the very next day, he walked up onto our front porch in Pasadena, rang the doorbell, and asked my parents if he could take me out to the movies."

Mel gasps. "What did he take you to see?"

"*Meet the Parents*," Mom says.

Neither of us get the reference.

"Ben Stiller at his finest," she says, pausing for signs of recognition from me and Mel. After a beat, she shrugs and gives up.

"As long as you had fun," Mel adds.

"We did!" Mom says.

Then she takes a deep breath.

I notice her grip on her coffee mug tighten and a strain fall across her facial features. I want to tell her that she doesn't have to keep talking if she doesn't want to. But I'm also dying to know what happened next. I know this boy she's talking about is *not* my dad. I know this because the two of them met when Dad's family moved from Michigan to SoCal because of his mom's job as a doctor. Dad was a senior in high school at the time, just like Mom. They were friends back then, but they didn't start dating until years later at the end of college. And then a few years after that, they had me and got married.

A pit forms in my stomach when it hits me that she's about to tell us how it all went wrong with this boy in high school. *And* who he was.

Mom clears her throat. "Me and this boy got very serious very fast. Too fast. It was puppy love, but at the time I was convinced he was going to be the love of my life. I couldn't see past the two of us being together forever."

"Okay, Mom. I can't take it," I cut in. "How did he mess things up?"

"Right. Because we know the boy messed things up," Mel says. "It's always the boy."

Mom laughs, and I'm relieved because for a second I thought she might start to cry.

"We just were young and dumb," she says. "It's as simple as that, honestly. We got into this big fight right before junior prom. I said some things. He said some things. I thought we'd be able to fix it, but I was wrong. He . . . um. I wasn't even convinced our breakup was real. I went to the dance alone, thinking he was going to do the same. I thought we'd figure things out over a slow dance to *NSYNC or something."

She laughs, but it's a sad one. "But when I showed up, he was there with Brittany Bostic."

"Wait, he was dancing with her? Or she was his date?" Mel asks.

Mom takes a sip of her coffee, then straightens, scratching the back of her neck. "His teal cummerbund and bow tie matched her dress perfectly," Mom says, and her tone has some bite to it. Her eyes are kind of distant, like she's remembering the exact visual as we speak.

She seems briefly lost in thought, so I clear my throat to get her attention. "Mom, did you talk to him that night?"

"No. I, uh . . . We didn't speak again after that," she admits. "Not until he bought a summer home on the east shore of the lake."

Mel gasps, putting everything together before I can catch up. "Simon Rodriguez was your first boyfriend!"

Mom nods.

"Mom, how are you only telling me this now?" I ask, jumping up from my stool.

"Well, honey," she says, motioning for me to sit back down, "I wanted to explain it to you the night your dad showed up. I knew you'd gotten the wrong idea from what you overheard. But you ran off in the rain with Tommy Ling." I gasp, because I could have sworn my lie worked. She winks at me and keeps talking. "I'm a mom. We know things."

And now I'm kicking myself because I've spent a week

thinking the worst of my mom. She never cheated on my dad. She just fell in love young and got her heart stomped on. Could she have told Dad about her and Simon years ago? Sure. But a girl's entitled to *some* secrets, I guess.

"Anyway," Mom continues, "I'm telling you this because you're the same age I was when I fell in love and got my heart broken for the first time. And . . . I think it would have been nice to have a mom to compare notes with back then." She pauses, curling her bottom lip into her mouth like she's considering something. "And also, I think you should go after Tommy. And I think I'm going with you."

Mel's mouth drops into an *O*, and I practically leap across the island to wrap my mom in a massive hug.

"What kind of mom lets her girl drive winding mountain roads at night alone?" she asks, circling her arms around me. Then she pulls back to look me in the eyes. "After all, it's not a 'grand gesture' if you don't make it in one piece."

CHAPTER THIRTY-ONE

Me: I need your help

Me: Plus u owe me

P: Facts. Everything ok?

Me: Yes but I need a HUGE favor

Patrick's typing bubble pops up, does a little dance, then disappears. My nerves are already shot to hell, and now I can hardly breathe. As if it wasn't hard enough for me to work up the nerve to go after Tommy, now I'm enlisting the help of his brother. I'm about to send Patrick another text when suddenly a video call comes through.

It's him.

I swipe open the call, attempting to appear calm and royally failing. "Patrick! Hey!"

By his background, I can tell he's in the movie room with Bekah. She smiles and waves at the camera while Patrick talks with a Red Vine hanging from his mouth. "Hey, Andie-Bug, so you need help with something?"

I don't miss the way he uses my nickname for the first time this summer. But I also don't have time to dwell on the spark of warmth that blooms in my chest either. Guess I'm officially not mad at him anymore. I especially won't be if he can come through for me now.

"Uh, yeah," I say, suddenly feeling queasy because I'm about to confess something major. "I need to explain something, though. You know how at Augie's party you mentioned how me and Tommy have been hanging out this summer?"

"Yep," he says. And he's so casual and unbothered, it's throwing me off a little bit.

"Well, turns out . . . I kind of fell for your brother. But I think he fell for me first. Then I seriously messed it all up, and now he's run off to meet up with Chloe and it's all my fault. So I need to know if you know where they're meeting so my mom can take me there and I can tell him how I feel."

I blurt this all out in one breath. When I finish, I'm panting. In the background, Bekah is beaming from ear to ear. Patrick's eyebrows practically meet his hairline, and his mouth drops into a massive *O*. Then, slow and steady, a smile creeps across his lips.

"Andie Weaver, I didn't think you had it in you," he says before the camera swoops and he starts tapping on the screen. Now I'm looking up at his five o'clock shadow and nostrils.

"Does that mean you're going to help me or—" Then I hear a *whoosh*.

"Just sent you a pin for the diner where he's meeting her," Patrick says. "I think you're right about him falling for you first, by the way."

A flood of relief washes over me. "I owe you big!"

"Nah, call it even," Bekah says, grabbing the phone from Patrick. "Now go get your man, girlfriend."

With how this summer started, I never thought it could actually end with me finding love. And by the way Mom is speeding down these winding mountain roads at night, that's still very much in question. At this rate, next year everyone could have the pleasure of visiting a plaque on the side of the road that reads ANDIE WEAVER WOULD DO ANYTHING FOR LOVE, EVEN PLUNGE TO HER DEATH ON THE WAY TO FIND IT.

I'm clutching the passenger-side door with one hand and the center console with the other. "Mom, you're good, right?"

"Mm-hmm," she hums. With the way the car makes a subtle swerve to the left, she's not convincing at all. "Sweetie, can you reach my purse in the back seat?"

Confused by this random request, I hesitate for a second. But figuring it's best she keep two hands on the wheel and both eyes forward, I do what she says. While reaching back I avoid looking out her window toward the guardrail and the rigid mountain line. And after tugging her enormous bag over the console and into my lap, I wait for more instructions.

"The letter in the side pocket," Mom says, "can you grab it for me?"

Blame it on the car sickness, but it's not until the piece of paper is in my hands that I fully realize that it isn't a utility bill or credit card offer Mom's looking for. It's the Letter I found in her top drawer on the Fourth of July.

For a second time, I turn the piece of paper over in my hands. The same blue ink bleeds through the page. "Mom, what's going on? Are we about to do some kind of release ritual where we tear this up and throw it off the mountain?"

Surprising me, she laughs. "No, honey. I *want* you to read it this time," she says, taking her eyes off the road for a split second to glance at what I'm sure are both my eyes bulging out of their sockets. "I think it's time." And when I just sit there frozen, she insists. "It's okay, sweetie. I promise."

I swallow hard and slowly unfold the piece of paper, holding my breath like the letter could be filled with anthrax. Then I read it in full.

I finish the letter, and for maybe the first time in my short life, I am truly speechless. Because now I'm picturing a seventeen-year-old Simon Rodriguez hunched over his kitchen counter, scribbling his heart out on a piece of loose-leaf paper for the girl of his dreams—and it just so happens that girl is my mom.

I reach up to swipe a tear from my eye, wondering how it got there and why I'm so emotional. "Why did you let me read this, Mom?"

She clears her throat but thankfully keeps her eyes on the road. "Because Simon Rodriguez wrote that letter when we were seventeen, but he didn't give it to me until earlier this summer."

I run through the calendar in my mind, and suddenly it all makes sense. "The day he showed up on our front porch?"

Mom nods as she steers the car with the bends of the road. "I don't know if getting this letter back then would have changed the course of history," she admits. "And trust me, Andie, I *don't* regret marrying your dad. We loved each other for a long time." She reaches across the console to squeeze my knee. "And you'd better believe I think the universe would have conspired to make you my daughter no matter the outcome. But best of all, your dad and I made you. You are the best parts of both of us but so uniquely yourself too."

Tracing my fingers over Simon's handwriting, I get stuck on a particular line: *I will never stop hoping that one day we'll get a chance to try again.* "Why do you think Simon waited all this time to give you this?" I ask.

Looking over at her, she's smiling a soft, somewhat sad smile. "He told me that back then he chickened out because he saw me at the batting cages with some guy one day after school and lost his nerve. After that, he just assumed trying with me was a lost cause."

"But now that you and Dad split up and Dad's getting remarried . . . ," I add on, and Mom shrugs.

"Who knows?" she says casually. "Can you believe the man delivered the letter and *still* didn't ask me out?"

"I've discovered that men are very confusing creatures," I tell her, which draws out a full-throated laugh. Still, none of this explains her timing. "Mom, why are you telling me this now? Why tonight?" I ask.

She signals for the exit to Arrowhead, which means we're getting close to the diner where Tommy's meeting Chloe. "Remember when I told you at the start of this summer that I wanted you to use this time to ask questions about yourself and try to find the answers?"

I nod.

"Simon and I ended things with a big question mark . . . No closure. And I want you to know that no matter the outcome of tonight with you and Tommy, you're going to be okay," she tells me. "Because either way, you're walking out of that diner with an answer."

"And this is what you wanted to talk to me about after Mel's shoot?" I ask, because when I got home, I made a beeline for my bedroom, and she spent most of the night texting me tips on how to get skunk smell out of 3B textured hair.

Mom nods. "I saw your face when you came downstairs and found Tommy in the entryway," she tells me. "And I saw how you immediately shut down all those feelings to play it cool. I felt like I was looking at a version of myself from twenty-five years ago."

"So what you're saying is," I cut in, "you want me to be brave?"

She nods again. "And if it crashes and burns—which it might—I'll be here to pick up the pieces."

I reach across and grab her hand to squeeze it tight.

When Mom and I pull into the parking lot of the Cedar Glen Inn diner, my anxiety is in overdrive, and I can't tell if my heart is lodged in my throat or my butt. Since we took the exit, I almost asked her twice to pull over so I could dry-heave on the side of the road. The last time I was this nervous, I was standing thirty feet up on a rock face about to free-fall into a still body of water. But then I at least had Tommy holding my hand.

Mom parks and shuts off the engine. We sit in silence for several seconds while I give myself a silent pep talk. *You can do this. Worst-case scenario, they're making out in a booth and you'll just eat your feelings in the next one over.*

"Do you want me to go in and sit at a table in a corner for moral support?" Mom asks, interrupting my nightmare visual.

I shake my head. "Mm-mm. Nope. I'm a big girl. I can do this," I tell her. But mostly I'm just trying to convince myself.

Then I remember that Mel requested minute-by-minute

updates. So I grab my phone and tap out a text: Just parked. Going in.

Her reply is instant.

Mel: YOU GOT THIS BETCH

Mel: REAL HOT GIRL SHIT

Mel: But fr. ILY YGT 😗

Smiling at my best friend's theatrics, I slide my phone back into my pocket and reach for the door handle. I tell my mom I love her, and then I'm off to get my answer.

From the outside, the diner looks pretty empty. I expected to see Tommy and Chloe sitting and talking in a booth. My plan was to send him a text, then wait for a response. I figured that would create less of a scene than me stomping up to their table like a scorned mistress with a freshly positive pregnancy test. At the same time, I didn't think this all the way through. Because now I'm just lurking *outside* the diner like a creeper. I'm about to give up and return to the car when I hear my name.

"Andie?"

Chills break out across my arms even though it's eighty degrees, and I turn to find Tommy standing a few feet away. Alone.

His summer tan is a deep bronze against a white UCLA T-shirt and matching shorts. And his floppy hair shines in the parking lot lights.

He asks the obvious. "What are you doing here?"

Maybe it's nerves, or he just looks *that* good, but it takes a beat for me to find my voice. "I needed to talk to you."

"How did you find me?" Another very reasonable question.

"Ummm . . . I'd rather not reveal my sources," I say, just in case Chloe's in the bathroom waiting for him to come back in and this turns into a bad soap opera. It's best if I don't incriminate anyone else.

"Oh-kaaay," he says, stuffing his hands into his pockets to pull out his phone. "Sorry, did I miss an SOS text or something? I've been kind of—"

"No, no!" I cut him off and rush to explain. "It's not that. I didn't come here because of the arrangement. In fact, I want to cancel the arrangement."

His eyebrows scrunch together, and he sucks in his lips, like he has no idea what's going on here. I decide to enlighten him.

"Tommy, I'm here because I need to set the record straight. I don't want to be your emotional-support animal anymore," I say. "I mean . . . I do still want to support you emotionally. But I also want to kiss you, and hold your hand, and jump off rocks with you, and watch old movies—good ones and bad ones—with you. And I want to read your drafts and let you read mine. And I want to watch you play baseball, or *not* play baseball. Whatever you decide to do. I want to be your friend *and* your girlfriend. Your emotional-support girlfriend. Also, I backed out of the dare because I freaked out and I was scared after last summer on the beach with Patrick. But with you, I can jump off rocks. And I don't know what's going on with you and Chloe. But please don't go into that diner. Please don't go back to her. She didn't know a good thing when she had you. And I don't technically *have* you right now. But I know you're a good thing. Pig. Gerbil. Person—you know what I mean."

I pause and take a deep breath. I'm rambling, and the more I talk, the more confused Tommy appears. Still, he takes a few steps toward me. "Chloe's gone," he says. "She was here, but she left."

"Oh."

"She left when I told her about you."

"*Oh.*"

"I need to set the record straight too," he says, walking closer. I'm buzzing with anticipation, but I take a moment to appreciate the way the moonlight highlights his cheekbones. "And I'm going to do it Andie-style, so buckle up. I kissed you on that boat because I'd *been* wanting to for weeks. For the record, I'd kiss you anywhere. In front of our stupid friends or in a dark alley. And I agreed to be your emotional-support animal because I've spent three summers being *just* your neighbor when I should have always been your friend. And now we have a chance to be more, and I want that with you. Most importantly, I only agreed to meet Chloe today because I thought we both needed closure for us to move on. But all it took was me saying your name out loud for her to realize that I already had."

Apparently, I'm a broken record, because all I can say to all of that is, "Oh."

"And another thing," he says, stepping closer. So close that I can feel his warmth against my chest. He looks down at me with those deep green eyes. "I don't want you comparing me to Patrick."

"Tommy, there is no comparison. There never was," I say, meaning every word. Hoping I don't fall all over myself with what I'm about to say next—and that if I do, he'll be there to catch me—I take a deep breath and dive. "Because I can't kiss you just once and then never again."

The corners of his mouth turn up in a slow spreading smile, and before I know it, he's full-on beaming at me—dimples popping, eyes crinkled at the sides. That whole-faced smile that makes the air even thinner than it already was up here.

"You did it, Andie Weaver. You jumped first," he says, brushing my bangs out of my eyes. It's the first time he's touched me since I got here. And it feels like his fingertips are capable of magic.

I nod, laughing. "Yeah, I guess so," I say as his face inches closer to mine and his hands curve around the small of my back.

He lifts a hand to tangle his fingers into the curls at the back of my neck, positioning my head for what we both know is coming next. My chest flutters and my stomach does a flip. If I thought I knew what it meant before to feel butterflies, I was wrong. Because *this* is it, right here, a whole sanctuary of them.

"Let's just say we jumped together," I tell him before his lips fall into perfect alignment with mine. And maybe there are no real fireworks for my second kiss with Tommy Ling, but it doesn't matter. Because I have a feeling there will be plenty more chances for that.

"Mom, that color looks *insane* on you." I just walked into her bathroom as she's getting ready for a blind date with a doctor she met on the kind of app you have to apply for—only the best for my mom.

His name is Michael, and of course I ran my full-scale amateur FBI background scan on him the second he asked her out. I'm not looking to have her on one of those *How I Fell in Love and Got Scammed* streaming docs anytime soon.

"Thanks, Andie Bug," she says, swishing her hips in the deep purple frilly dress she's put on for their dinner, a major upgrade from the soft pants she's worn all summer.

"What do you kids have planned for the night?"

Leaning against the doorframe, I fiddle with the charm bracelet on my left wrist. It's the one that got tangled in Mrs. Ling's wig at the start of the summer. I thought it was a lost cause, but yesterday I got a text from Tommy instructing me to check my front porch. And there it was resting on the wood railing. I picked it up and felt a buzz in my pocket. It was a text from Tommy, who had been watching me from his house. Notice anything different? he asked. And that's when I saw the extra charm—a tiny pink pig, of the emotional-support variety. Instantly I set off to cross the lawn between our houses. A small smile creeps across my lips now, just thinking about it. Mom clears her throat.

"Hello, Earth to Andie!"

"Sorry! Just an innocent game night over at Mason's," I tell her. But I don't miss the way her eyes shoot up to meet mine in the vanity, at the mention of Simon Rodriguez's house.

"Oh," Mom says, a flush rushing to her warm brown cheeks. Now she's casually fiddling with her mascara, although she's already swiped it several times. "Well, please tell his dad I say hello."

"I'll definitely do that," I say, trying to mask my smile.

Although, he won't be there. Because what I *don't* tell my mom is that the reason we picked Mason's house is because tonight it's completely parent-free.

I wanted to skip and spend the night in Tommy's movie

room—I'd like to actually watch *Never Been Kissed* before I graduate. But it's our last night with everyone at the lake, so we're banding together for a final hurrah. Augie suggested paintball. When the entire group chat replied with tomato emojis and various GIFs, Mason offered up his dad's house for game night.

My phone buzzes at my hip.

Tommy: be down to pick u up in 5

Me: can't believe I'm doing this . . . again 😵

Tommy: don't worry

Tommy: I've got you

Me: ♥

"You can do this, babe!" Tommy whispers into my car. It's been three days since we kissed in a diner parking lot, and he's been calling me that ever since—like he's waited to call me that for *much* longer. I don't think it'll ever get old.

But there's no time for me to swoon because right now I'm staring into frothy blond liquid sloshing in a Solo cup. And my stomach just did that lurching thing it does whenever confronted with the prospect of digesting hops.

Bekah's just sunk another Ping-Pong ball into her target cup on our side, and it's my turn to drink.

"I so *can't* do this," I say, looking up into Tommy's eyes.

"Drink! Drink! Drink! Drink!" everyone's chanting. Everyone but Mel and Tommy, who exchange a look of mutual concern.

"Who's got the bucket?" Evan shouts.

"Maybe give Tommy your turn," Bekah suggests. She's gone a bit lax since the start of the summer.

For some reason, that's what emboldens me to raise the cup to my lips. This summer I've done big things. Gotten over heartbreak, humiliation, a fear of heights. Even gone after the boy and got him. What's a cup of beer got on me?

I close my eyes and tip it back.

Everyone's quiet, as if waiting for me to double over. When I set the cup down and raise my arms in triumph, they all cheer. Tommy lifts me from behind and spins me around. He sets me down, and I turn to him, beaming.

"What did you do?" I whisper as we switch positions so he can prep for his turn.

He raises a finger to his lips. "Shhhh." Then he nods down to where he subtly kicks a carton under the table that's just barely obscured by other cartons of beer.

I bend down, pretending to tie my shoe so I can read the label. *It's ginger ale.*

I think I just fell even harder.

I stand up behind him, wrapping my arms around his waist as he sinks the ball into a cup on Patrick and Bekah's side of the table. "Thank you," I whisper into his back.

"Told you," he says, turning to kiss my hair. "I've got you."

And he does. He's got me this summer, next, and all the days in between.

ACKNOWLEDGMENTS

As a self-professed hopeless romantic and drama queen since age eight, diving into YA romance has been the most rewarding experience for me. There's something about those tender years of "almost" adulthood that make heartbreak and infatuation feel deeper and more earth-shatteringly grand. Expressing it all through Andie and Tommy's love story was the creative jolt I absolutely needed this year. So for that, I have many people to thank.

First, I'm always grateful to my fabulous literary agent, Kim Lionetti, without whom this opportunity may never have materialized. My editor, Jessi Smith, whose enthusiasm for these characters and my writing was like wind at my back. I'd also love to thank the many talented teams at Simon Pulse whose editing, production, and art design helped *You Jump First* reach its full potential.

On a personal note, I'm thankful to my family and friends, who've supported my writing dreams from the first page of the first draft of my debut novel, on through every outline and proposal I manage to dream up and soldier through. So thank you endlessly to . . .

My good friend, author Audrey Cleo Yap, who lent me inspiration for Tommy's middle name, Kai Le. The authors who encourage and inspire me via almost *daily* voice notes: Naina Kumar, Shirlene Obuobi, Ellie Palmer, and Danica Nava. My sister-friends: Caelayn, Lauren, Tawny, Allison F., Tanisha, and Chelsea. It's so good doing life with y'all! My *actual* sister, Faith, who turns all my books into book cakes and flies all over the country with me. And my son, Henry, who inspires me daily and is the reason I took this leap into writing in the first place.

Lastly, it only felt right to dedicate my first YA novel to three of my best friends from high school: Kelsey Riley, Amy Westlake, and Allison Rhodes. The world throws a lot at you in this life. But if you can manage to hang on to true friendships along the way, you're absolutely doing something right.